PRAISE FOR E.L. CHEN

"*Sweetside Motel* is a terrifying and totally engaging modern Gothic, ending in a pitch-perfect finale."

—DEVAN BARLOW, AUTHOR OF THE CURSES & CURTAINS SERIES

"Immersive and captivating, E. L. Chen's *Sweetside Motel* is unbearably tense and refuses to let you go. An unputdownable exploration of how abuse changes the human psyche in a pandemic hit world, it felt like it seeped into my soul. One of my favourite reads of the year."

—SARAH NEW, AUTHOR OF *AMISSIS LIBERIS* AND *HYPOCHONDRIA*

"This dark, atmospheric book has all the initial hallmarks of a classic gothic novel, updated for modern times. And indeed, it is that. But it is also something stranger and more unexpected—a twisty psychological thriller with plot turns I couldn't predict, where no one and nothing is quite what it seems, and with complicated characters who are by turns charming, endearing, surprising, and horrific. I loved it. If you decide to follow Sarah on her road trip to (and *from*) darkness, buckle up and be prepared for the ride."

—VANESSA FOGG, AUTHOR OF *THE HOUSE OF ILLUSIONISTS AND OTHER STORIES*

SWEETSIDE MOTEL

E.L. CHEN

This is a work of fiction. All of the characters, organizations, and events portrayed are either products of the author's imagination or used fictitiously.

SWEETSIDE MOTEL

Copyright © 2026 by E.L. Chen. All rights reserved.

No part of this book may be reproduced in any form or by any electronic or mechanical means, including information storage and retrieval systems, without written permission from the author and publisher, except for the use of brief quotations in a book review.

Edited by Holly Lyn Walrath.

Cover design by Holly Lyn Walrath.

Published by Interstellar Flight Press, Houston, Texas.

www.interstellarflightpress.com

ISBN (eBook): 978-1-953736-52-9

ISBN (Paperback): 978-1-953736-53-6

First Edition: 2026

SWEETSIDE MOTEL

CONTENTS

Chapter One	1
Chapter Two	3
Chapter Three	13
Chapter Four	23
Chapter Five	33
Chapter Six	41
Chapter Seven	51
Chapter Eight	59
Chapter Nine	65
Chapter Ten	69
Chapter Eleven	77
Chapter Twelve	85
Chapter Thirteen	93
Chapter Fourteen	101
Chapter Fifteen	111
Chapter Sixteen	119
Acknowledgments	123
About the Author	125
Interstellar Flight Press	127

Content warnings: Child abuse (off-page), death of a parent, domestic abuse, emotional abuse, infidelity, murder, racism, suicide and suicidal ideation, violence

CHAPTER ONE

Drive. Drive as fast as you can, as far away as you can. Drive until horses and hay bales wink by on the side of the road instead of industrial plazas and big box malls. Drive until the only radio station you can reach on the dial crackles in French. Drive until you can't feel your fingers wrapped around the steering wheel, and when you wash your hands in the rest stop bathroom, you trace the faux-leather stitches branded into your palms. Drive until the blood on your hooded sweatshirt dries, and you can pretend it was only a nosebleed.

Drive even though it's started to snow, and you never did put on your winter tires. Because skidding across two lanes of highway at a hundred kilometers an hour into the exposed bedrock of the Canadian Shield is better than anything waiting for you back in Toronto.

Just drive, until you can't anymore.

CHAPTER TWO

The car breaks down half an hour outside of Sweetside. Literally. The sign at the side of Highway 11 taunts *Sweetside 50*. Sarah pops the hood in its shadow and swipes wet clumps of snow off her eyelashes, studying the hatchback's steaming innards as if she knows what she's looking at. Craggy slopes of rock topped with snow-capped conifers press in from both sides of the road, compacting her anxiety into diamond-hard edges. She's a long way from Toronto's glass and steel and concrete.

A tractor-trailer snarls past, shaking the little hatchback and sending Sarah stumbling from the highway's gravelly shoulder into the ditch. "Stupid, stupid," she mutters as she climbs back up, the near-frozen mud biting into the soles of her sneakers. Why did she think getting away would be easy?

A black and white cruiser pulls up behind the hatchback and parks. Bile rises in the back of Sarah's throat. They can't have found her already. She buttons up the neck of her peacoat with cold-numbed fingers and flips up the collar to hide her stained hoodie.

The officer who climbs out of the car is a tall, burly white man whose mask barely contains his greying beard. Sarah suddenly feels naked as the wind whips her bare cheeks. He looks her up and down. She guesses he's cataloguing her surface traits: her hair's severe black gloss, her skin extra pale and sallow from months spent indoors, and her eyes. It always comes down to the eyes. Ben once compared her to a Modigliani portrait, which wasn't the compliment he thought it was.

"You're far from home, miss," the officer says, very loudly and slowly, having come to the usual conclusion.

Sarah forces a smile. "I was on my way to see my brother in Timmins." She hopes the officer doesn't expect her to prove this. Graham isn't expecting her, and she's not sure if he'd welcome visitors during a pandemic.

He blinks. "Can I see some ID?" he says, this time a little faster.

"It's in the car."

Sarah opens the passenger door of the hatchback with shaking hands, trying to remember everything her Black friends ever told her about being pulled over by the cops. "I'm getting my wallet," she calls out over the hammering of her heart.

The officer, thankfully, doesn't flinch when her hand disappears into the backpack on the front seat. Her fingers glance off the knife's crusty handle, and she hastily pushes it beneath her water bottle and change of clothes.

She pulls out her wallet, places it on the roof of the car, and backs away. The officer opens the wallet, his eyebrows lifting at the amount of cash she's carrying. "Sarah. That's an unusual name."

"Really?"

"Well, for you, eh?" he says, and Sarah fights to keep the smile on her face. "Where're you from?"

"Toronto."

He sniffs. "That's just as bad."

"As bad as what?"

"You know," the officer says, and she does. "It's not a good time to go visiting."

"My brother lives by himself, and—and so do I."

He places the wallet back on the roof of the car. "I'll call you a tow truck."

"Thank you."

He looks her up and down again. "Don't thank me yet," he says, and unease shrinks her stomach into a knot.

The officer ambles back to his car and sits inside, bringing a cell phone to his ear. Sarah scoops up her wallet and drops it in the backpack.

The snow is either coming down heavier or blowing off the scraggly trees perched on the rocks. Sarah huddles on her hatchback's passenger seat against the numbing cold and dread. There's nothing she can do but wait for the outcome of a stranger's phone call.

She continues to smile, in case the officer is watching.

She feels smaller than she's ever felt before, dwarfed by the rock outcroppings and the grey highway that stretches on forever. When she'd started out, the highway had promised freedom. The unknown hadn't seemed as vast and scary. She'd been excited to see so many trees. Sometimes, as she drove, sunlight would catch on a creek or pond, a glittering oasis tucked in the woods. And then the trees would spring up again, and the water would disappear like a daydream. Just a lovely secret revealed to drivers who happened to glance out the passenger window at the right place and time.

Now, standing still, the trees reveal nothing. The shaggy conifers cower under a veil of falling snow. The grey sky leeches the color out of everything, leaving only the grimy tint of salted slush splashed on the underskirts of her hatchback.

The officer has been off his phone for a while, writing in a tiny notebook. The blood roars in Sarah's ears, or maybe it's another truck rattling past. They'll be looking for her. And this officer will remember her. Of course he will. He won't remember her face, but he'll remember what she looks like. The box she ticks.

A muddy tow truck materializes out of the falling snow and pulls up behind the police car. The officer gets out to greet the driver. A rangy young white man bounds from the truck, his mask tucked under his chin.

Sarah reluctantly climbs back out into the cold. The tow truck driver glances up at the sudden movement and yanks the mask up over his nose. "Shit," he says, stepping back. Sarah's teeth grind behind her smile. "Are you fucking kidding me, Isaac? She could have the virus."

"She's from Toronto," the officer says.

"Exactly."

"We can't leave the car on the side of the highway, Jerry. It's a traffic hazard."

"Fine. I'll take the car, but not her. Lars'll probably quarantine it for a few days before he touches it."

Panic surges in Sarah's chest like heartburn. "A few *days?*"

Jerry blinks at her in surprise and then turns back to the officer. "So she's gonna need someplace to stay."

"I could call my brother—" she starts.

"Timmins is almost six hours away, and it'll be dark soon. And you can't ask him to drive in this." The officer gestures at the flurrying snow, and Sarah's legs threaten to buckle, because he's right.

"She can't come to town," Jerry says, twitching like a rabbit. "The inn's closed, and no one's doing Airbnb anymore. And even if they were, no one's gonna take *her*."

"I haven't been anywhere but the grocery store for months, and I always mask up," Sarah says, struggling to keep her smile in place. "I don't have COVID."

Jerry spits on the gravel. "We don't know that. Shit, *you* don't know that."

"Is there anywhere I can go?" she asks, trying to keep dismay from cracking her polite surface.

The officer shakes his head. "Every place around here is closed. Though I could ask—" He clicks his tongue.

Jerry smirks. "The Suicide Motel?"

The officer shoots him a look that could sear glass. "My nephews run a motel just outside of town. They're closed too, but I could ask them to put you up. They had good reviews before—" He waves his hand, as if *before* is another place, like the city Sarah just left. "You'll have to quarantine for two weeks before we let you in town to get your car."

"But my brother could pick me up tomorrow—"

The officer's eyes narrow above his mask. "I don't know what it's like in Toronto—" The name of her hometown comes out as a sneer, and she realizes with a sinking heart that being from the big bad city is another mark against her. "But in Sweetside, we take the pandemic seriously. Half our seniors died, including my in-laws, and a bunch more folks are on ventilators in North Bay. So no one comes through unless they've got a clean bill of health. I hope you don't have anywhere to be."

Sarah's face is starting to ache from smiling. "No. Not at all."

Sarah's sneakers skid over the frosty gravel of the highway's shoulder. Although she's found her mask and put it on, Jerry still won't come within ten feet of her. She places the car key on the driver's seat and steps away to give him space, fighting hopeless tears. That key was her key to freedom. The key to the future. But she'd been foolish to think she deserved one. And now here she is, dependent on—as the Tennessee Williams play says—the kindness of strangers.

She doesn't remember *A Streetcar Named Desire* ending well for Blanche.

She fists her bare hands in her coat's pockets, shrinking every time a blob of snow deposits a sloppy kiss on her ears. Her mask's cotton layers aren't enough to block the wind's icy claws, and she's frozen inside and out. The police officer is on the phone again, inside his car. He doesn't make eye contact with her, and neither does Jerry. The tow truck driver hooks up her car, and the blinking rear of the old hatchback disappears into the horizon. Sarah watches forlornly as snow fills in the tire tracks. Minutes later, there's little evidence her car ever existed. She'd wanted to disappear, but not like this.

A red pickup does a U-turn and pulls in behind the police car. A stack of plywood juts out of the back, covered loosely with a tarp.

The officer climbs out of his car and beckons at Sarah. "That's Caleb, my nephew."

Sarah peers at the truck, trying to make out her savior through the blowing snow and swaying windshield wipers. Another white man sits behind the wheel, his shoulders filling out a red buffalo plaid jacket. A wing of dark brown hair falls over his forehead as he grabs the mask dangling from the rearview mirror. She catches a glimpse of a square chin dimpled with a cleft before it disappears beneath the fabric.

"Uncle Isaac," the man calls out as he hops down from the truck. Although they're both masked, Sarah can see the family resemblance. The height, the broad shoulders, the purposeful way they move. These are men who never have to think about how much space they take up because they're used to people making room for them.

Although her jaw aches, Sarah plasters on another smile, hoping it reaches her eyes as most of her face is covered. Unlike the officer and the tow truck driver, Caleb doesn't seem surprised by her appearance. He regards her steadily with deep-set blue eyes that never drop below her neck.

"Caleb, this is Miss—I can't pronounce her last name. This is Sarah."

"Welcome to Sweetside, Sarah." The corners of Caleb's eyes crinkle, and Sarah imagines his square jaw smiles with very straight, very white teeth. "Let's get you in the truck. You must be freezing."

"Remember, Miss Sarah, you're not to leave the motel for two weeks. I'll be checking up on you. Don't make us board you in." The officer thumps the plywood in the back of the truck.

With his mask on, she can't tell if he's joking. She nods, her mouth dry. Caleb opens the passenger-side door for her, and she climbs into the cab. There's no going back now, but there was no going back hours ago when she got into her car and started driving.

Caleb slams the door and waves at the police officer, then gets into the driver's seat. Sarah hugs her backpack to hide the frightened staccato of her heart. For months, it had only been her and Ben in 650 square feet, and now she's trapped in a tiny space with a man again.

After Caleb pulls off onto the highway, he turns up the heat in the truck. Sarah whimpers gratefully as her toes begin to thaw. "I couldn't help noticing you're not dressed for the weather," he says.

He's so close that Sarah can feel his voice vibrating inside her ribcage. She hugs the backpack tighter. "It wasn't snowing in Toronto when I left," she lies. She'd been in such a hurry to flee that she'd stuffed her feet into the first pair of shoes by the door.

She tries to calculate if she has enough cash to pay for the motel as well as food delivery. They might trace her cards. "What's your nightly rate?"

"Don't worry about it. We're paying for hydro anyway until the end of the month. Heat's gotta stay on so the pipes don't freeze, so it doesn't make a difference to us if you're there to enjoy it."

"Thank you. That's very kind." She's not used to kindness. *Kindness* sends her arms tensing around her backpack, wondering if the truck is going too fast for her to jump out of it.

Caleb smirks. "Don't think I'm a saint. It's also out of guilt. I'm guessing Uncle Isaac gave you a hard time. I bet Jerry was an asshole, too." He shakes his head. "Sweetside was paranoid about strangers even before the pandemic. And I imagine since you're—" He waves his hand toward her.

"You don't care that I'm Chinese?" she says lightly. Smile. Make it a joke, so they don't think you're accusing them of anything.

"I went to college in Toronto. I know there's a world outside Sweetside. And," he adds, the corners of his eyes crinkling again, "I don't get my news from the comments section."

She relaxes a little, but the sooner she gets behind a locked door, the better. Caleb's friendliness could still be an act. She's well-acquainted with deceptive charm.

"So, tell me about yourself, Sarah," Caleb says. "What do you do?"

"I'm a freelance writer. Mostly marketing copy, and some editing."

"Oh, that's good. So you won't have been affected much by the lockdown."

He doesn't notice her smile waver.

The town sign emerges from behind the snow on the side of the road. WELCOME TO SWEETSIDE POPULATION 1,500. Someone has spray-painted STAY OUT underneath in furious red strokes, and Sarah feels like they've written the message specifically for her.

Caleb sighs. "Well, I'm sorry you're not experiencing the best hospitality Sweetside has to offer. Here we are."

A low-slung shape appears ahead. A roadside motor inn, the mainstay of tourist routes that predates hotel franchises and loyalty programs. Sarah passed many of them during her flight up Highway 11. It made her nostalgic for the road trips she'd taken as a kid through cottage country, Ba-Ba at the wheel of the car, Ma-Ma flipping through the Ontario tourism guidebook with all the accommodations within their price range highlighted. Sarah and Graham would sit in the back, separated by the picnic cooler. At the time, she'd never noticed anything unusual. Now she wonders if the locals peered at her family with the same suspicion as Jerry and Officer Isaac. Maybe that was why Ba-Ba preferred motels to hotels, because you never have to pass other people in a hallway.

Caleb takes the next exit, rumbling off the road into the deserted parking lot. To Sarah's relief, the motel is not actually called the Suicide Motel. An unlit monolith of a sign proclaims *Sweetside Motel* in a retro script. Below it, black movable letters spell out CLOSED UNTIL FURTHER NOTICE STAY SAFE.

The building itself is single-story, cast from the same mold as the motels Sarah remembers staying at as a child. White aluminum siding stained grey by the darkening sky, the peaked roof crusted with snow. Each unit is marked by an orange door and a concrete planter filled with frosted, dead flowers. It might have been cheerful, if not for the frigid weather and air of abandonment.

"I'm afraid wifi's been turned off, but otherwise, everything's still on. You came just at the right time," Caleb says, and Sarah fights off a bitter laugh. "In a couple weeks, the water will be shut down too. We thought about keeping it open, but our housekeeper's in the hospital, and I don't think anyone will be taking advantage of ski season this winter anyway." He parks the truck and twists the key out of the ignition. It jangles against a half-dozen other keys as he hooks the carabiner keychain on his belt loop.

"Are you sure I can't pay you?" She doesn't want to be indebted to anyone, especially now.

"Oh, don't worry about us." He climbs out of the truck and comes around to the passenger side to open her door. Sarah clambers down, ready to run from this too-considerate man if she has to.

"We don't really need the money," he says, and then she sees the house.

The house lurks a little distance behind the motel, on a rising slope crowned by tall trees. In the fading twilight, Sarah makes out red brick, high gables, and gingerbread trim. The number of gables betrays that the house is large, but beneath the imposing pines, it resembles a dollhouse.

A hulking silhouette stands in a lighted window on the second floor. The hairs on the back of Sarah's neck lift, and it's not just from the cold.

She turns back to Caleb, a question in her eyes. He nods. "My brother Elijah and I live up there."

Sarah looks up at the house again. It's now completely dark. The tension in her abdomen spasms, releasing a nervous titter. "You don't have a dead mother in the basement, do you?" She regrets the joke as soon as it slips out of her mouth.

Caleb scratches his head. "Well, a boy's best friend *is* his mother."

He chuckles at her startled expression. "I'm joking! She's buried in the Sweet family plot on the other side of town. She passed away from cancer when I was a kid."

Thank goodness Sarah's mask hides her burning face. "Oh my God. I'm sorry."

"It's all right; it was a long time ago. Come on."

He picks another key from the cluster hanging from the carabiner and unlocks the door to the darkened motel office. Sarah hangs back in the doorway while Caleb flicks on a light and slips behind the reception desk. The office looks like it closed decades ago, instead of earlier this year. Wood paneling lines the walls, and a brown leather loveseat slouches below a Robert Bateman print of a wolf. The only modern touch is a painting hanging on the wall behind the desk. Black conifers crowd the large canvas, the brushstrokes unsettling in their violence.

"How about lucky number seven?" Caleb grabs a key hanging on a pegboard, an actual metal key with a red diamond-shaped tag. "All our units have a mini-fridge and a kettle. I can pick up groceries for you tomorrow if you want to make a list. You okay for tonight, though? I can bring you a sandwich."

It's a nice thing to do. Sarah shrinks back as he comes out from behind the desk. *Nice* can be taken away at the drop of a hat. *Nice* makes it more devastating when they turn on you, teeth bared. *Nice* is how they control you.

Sarah's stomach is hollow, though not from hunger. "I'm good, thanks."

Caleb leads her to a unit in the middle of the building. He unlocks and then holds the door open, and she sucks in her breath to make herself smaller as she squeezes past. He's a big man, taller than Ben and wider in the shoulders. All the more reason for her to not appear threatening.

The room smells faintly of bleach and the burned musk of an electric baseboard heater. Caleb flips a switch by the door, and a floor lamp flickers to life. They could be in any two-star motel in the country. Two double beds in matching salmon-and-jade bedspreads. Cream-colored lampshades on brass fixtures. Simple wooden furniture, all of which are stained the same shade of amber. The anonymous familiarity is comforting.

Like the office, the only modern touch other than the flatscreen TV is the paintings hanging above each bed. The canvases are only a couple feet square, but the painted pines seem to burst out of the edges. In the lamplight, the paint appears almost sculptural, as if the trees are made of thick black tongues. The brutal energy of the brushstrokes is dizzying. Sarah feels that if she were to touch the surface of the canvas, the trees would drag her into their depths.

"Think about what you might need for two weeks and let me know." Caleb reaches into his jacket and pulls out a business card. He hands it to her, along with the room key. SWEETSIDE MOTEL, the card says. YOUR NORTHERN GETAWAY. "The number will reroute to the house. Feel free to call anytime. One of us is always up."

"Thank you," Sarah says, laying a hand over her heart. If she appears sufficiently grateful, he'll leave, and she can take off her coat and wash the blood-stiff fleece scratching her breastbone.

He takes his weight off the door. Sarah instinctively holds it open and watches him walk to the truck. Her body remembers doing the same whenever guests left her home. It's funny, the things the body remembers even though friends haven't visited for years, not since she met Ben.

As soon as Caleb is a safe distance away, he unhooks his mask and turns to face her. He's in his mid-thirties, a little older than Sarah, with a straight nose, square jaw, and wide cheekbones roughened with dark stubble. In the dusk, his blue eyes are so drained of color they're almost clear.

In short, he looks like the kind of man who rescues stranded women. Sarah tenses against the open door, the business card creasing in her cold fingers.

"Have a good night, Sarah," he says. She was right about how white and straight his teeth are.

The polite thing to do would be to reveal her own face and thank him again. But she's not ready to take the mask off. She wordlessly closes the door and slides the chain lock in place.

CHAPTER THREE

When the truck drives away, Sarah screams.

She tugs the blackout curtains closed, strips off her mask, and collapses face-down on the nearest bed. She screams and pounds her fists and feet, feeling the satisfying ricochet off the boxspring mattress. Her voice scrapes her windpipe until she realizes she's laughing. Laughing and crying.

She's finally alone.

When the squall of elation subsides, she wobbles to the bathroom. She washes her mask in the sink first, then takes the hoodie into the shower with her. The little paper-wrapped motel soap is harsh, and she scrubs herself and the hoodie raw. The blood spatter won't completely come out of the pink cotton fleece, but it fades enough that she can claim she'd splashed coffee on herself while driving.

After the shower, she puts on pajamas and checks her phone. No calls or messages, but no one has this number. The battery's at 2%. She digs through her backpack for the charging cable and comes up empty. Her stomach sinks. The last place she saw it was in her car's glove compartment, where she'd shoved it after plugging in the phone at the rest stop to check the news.

The bedside table holds a notepad and ballpoint pen with the motel's address printed on them. Graham's number is the only one in her contacts, and she scrawls it on the pad before the phone gives up the ghost. It's a piece of crap, but what can you expect from a cheap burner bought from the grocery store? She tears off the page and stuffs it and the dead phone into her backpack. First thing tomorrow morning, she'll call Graham, and hopefully roads will have been cleared and he can drive down. She doesn't care about Officer Isaac's threats or Caleb's kind promises. She has to keep moving. She has to disappear.

Caleb had said there was no wifi, so her laptop is also useless. It's a good thing she told her clients she was taking time off. When she'd gone freelance, she thought she would miss going into an office. It's turned out to be a blessing, and not just because of lockdown. There's no one to keep track of her. Not even Ben.

Not anymore.

She switches on the TV and finds a local CBC affiliate. The six o'clock news is on, but it's all stories about the pandemic. Businesses struggling, cases rising, vaccines not available in Canada for months yet. No one's looking for an Asian woman who fled Toronto earlier that day.

She retrieves the crusty paring knife from the bottom of her backpack and washes that in the sink, too.

There's no point in staying up. She turns off the TV and the bedside lamp and stretches defiantly in the middle of the bed.

It's too dark. Too quiet. The hoodie hanging in the shower drip-drip-drips into the tub, each droplet echoing like a gunshot, echoing the percussive beat of her heart. Outside, the wind howls like a living thing, screaming like she had earlier. The wail of someone seeking to disappear.

Sarah tosses and turns on the too-firm mattress. Her toes strain against the tucked sheets; she struggles to kick them out. The stale motel air is smothering, as thick as the blankets on the bed. As thick as the brushstrokes on the painting above her head. The wind shrieks, or maybe it's her own voice in her head.

Isn't this what she wanted? To be alone?

She sits up and turns the TV back on. Voices fill the room, and she drifts into sleep at last.

Sarah wakes with a start to the growl of an engine outside. Ben's home. Clammy sweat spreads across her skin like frost.

Then her fists close around flannel, and she remembers in a rush that she's not at home. There's no TV in their bedroom, after all, let alone one broadcasting colored bars. The engine still grumbles outside, though, in the motel parking lot. Sarah glances at the clock. It's one in the morning. Why would Caleb come back at this time of night?

She switches off the TV, plunging the room into darkness. If it's not Caleb, they'll think the motel is deserted. It's been snowing for hours, enough time to hide their footprints.

Light seeps from under the edge of the blackout curtains, paralyzing Sarah with fear. How many times has she lain in bed like this, dreading Ben coming home? The warning drone of the hatchback as it pulled in front of the house, the headlights brightening the front window of their ground-floor apartment. Not knowing if he'd come in angry or sullen or affectionate. Not knowing if he'd come in at all, or fall asleep on the sofa texting some mystery woman, claiming the next morning he didn't want to wake Sarah up.

A car door slams. Raucous laughter breaches the darkness. "Over here!" a man yells. It doesn't sound like Caleb.

Sarah fumbles for the telephone on the bedside table. Who is she going to call? Not the police, they won't come for her. Not unless she leaves the motel and wanders up to town with the virus she's supposedly carrying. Her eyes fall on Caleb's business card, illuminated by the light leaking into the room. YOUR NORTHERN GETAWAY, it promises. Someone's getaway. Not hers. Hands shaking, she dials the number.

She almost sobs with relief when it picks up after the third ring. "Hello?" It's a male voice, lacking Caleb's deep resonance.

"Hi," she croaks. "Is Caleb there? It's Sarah at the motel."

"Do you hear them? Do you hear the screaming?"

"What?"

"*Elijah!*" a muffled voice hisses.

"It's the girl at the motel," the unfamiliar voice says.

There's a rattle and scrape as the receiver changes hands. "Hi, Sarah," Caleb says. "Is there a problem?"

She wants to cry at how calm and steady his voice is. "Sorry to call so late, but there are people outside and—"

She shrieks at the sudden explosion.

It's not a big explosion, like a bomb. Just a burst of concentrated violence, followed by a shimmer of sound, incongruous in its delicacy.

"Sarah?"

"They're breaking the—"

A smash bursts right in her eardrums, punctuated by more laughter and the tinkle of glass. The room suddenly sucks in a gust of freezing air, the blackout curtains lurching.

Sarah drops the receiver and rockets off the bed to the bathroom. Bare feet slapping the cold tile, she slams the door and locks it. The shouts and smashing glass suddenly sound far away, although not far enough. She snatches her knife off the counter, and for the second time in twenty-four hours, she's glad it's close.

She slides down to the floor, pressing her shoulder blades into the door to stop herself from shaking. *Do you hear them?* Elijah had asked. She wonders who *they* are. *Do you hear the screaming?* She hears nothing now except the familiar roar of blood rushing in her ears.

She's not sure how long she's been sitting in darkness when a thumping echoes in the distance. Someone's at the motel room door. She squeezes the knife handle, prepared to swipe, her lungs threatening to burst like she's spent too long underwater.

"Sarah!" a man shouts. "Sarah, are you in there?"

It's Caleb. She scrambles to her feet and hastily wraps the knife in a motel washcloth.

"Sarah?"

She darts out of the bathroom. A key scrapes in the lock as she stuffs the knife at the bottom of her bag. Her chest tightens, her legs tense. Will he be angry? Will he be sullen? Will he be affectionate?

"Sarah, I'm opening the door, okay? I just want to check if you're all right."

Caleb. It's only Caleb. Not Ben. "Coming!" she calls out.

She turns on the light and picks her way around the broken glass glittering on the carpet, praying she doesn't cut her feet open. The door jams on the chain lock. Caleb swears. "Hang on, I'll get it," she says. She slides the lock. The door bursts open, and winter wind slices through her pajamas to her already goose-bumped skin.

Caleb's masked figure fills the doorway, backlit by his truck headlights. He's holding a parka and a pair of lace-up boots. Sarah suddenly realizes she's not wearing a mask. He's seen her face now.

"Fuckers squealed out of here as soon as they saw me driving down." His fists clench in the parka's faux-fur hood.

"Who were they?"

"Hard to say with their masks on. Jerry or someone at the garage must've said something. They broke the windows in every unit. You're going to have to come up to the house."

"No, it's—"

The intensity in his eyes cuts her off. Her heart pounds, telling her to run, either away from or toward him.

"Here." Caleb thrusts out the parka and boots, and Sarah's resolve crumbles. Nice wins, at least tonight. "They're Elijah's. He's smaller than me." She pulls on a pair of clean socks while he replaces the phone receiver in its cradle. Her feet swim in the boots, and the coat smells alarmingly masculine, like cedar and paint thinner.

"Got anything in the bathroom?"

"Wait—" she starts, but he's already crossing the carpet. He returns with her damp mask and hoodie. She lunges for the hoodie, afraid he'll question the bloodstain, but he doesn't break his stride. He sweeps the door key from the dresser, and she has no choice but to stuff the rest of her things in her backpack.

Caleb holds the door open and takes the backpack as she passes. In the parking lot, tire tracks etch the amber-spattered snow. She can't tell if it's beer or urine, or both. Caleb locks the door to the unit and says, "Go straight to the truck. No, don't look back."

"What?" She looks; she can't help it.

Someone has spray-painted CHINK VIRUS on the door in fierce red letters.

Caleb exhales. "Fuck. I'm sorry."

"It's okay." Sarah swallows. She has no history with the word itself. All of her racist experiences in Toronto have been micro-aggressions, like Officer Isaac commenting on her name. Digs so subtle she can never be sure if she imagined them or not. Story of her life.

But the overtness of this hate stuns her. In Sweetside, the wolves don't bother with sheep's clothing, and she's not sure which is worse. She's read the news stories of increasing racist attacks, yes, but they always seem to happen outside her comfortable boundaries. Outside the city, outside the province, outside the country.

An itch spreads between her shoulder blades, reminding her she's wearing a target she can't take off, can't hide with makeup or clothing. Being female and Asian, she has to wear masks of a different kind. A friendly, innocent smile. Clothes that don't draw too much attention. A casual speech pattern, dropping the Gs from her verbs and softening her Ts, to show she's not one of *them*. She's from Toro*nn*o, not Toron*t*o, and she was headin' to Timmins to visit her bro. She's harmless. Not worth the trouble.

It's like living with Ben all over again.

"No, it's not okay." Caleb stalks over to the truck and opens the passenger door for her.

Sarah's reflexes kick in, and she feels the need to smooth his temper's jagged edges. "It is, really. No one's ever called me that before. It just makes me laugh. Like, seriously, what decade are we living in?"

"The current one, unfortunately. Here." Caleb thrusts her hoodie and mask into her hands, thankfully too rankled to scrutinize them. She hooks the elastic over her ears, and her shoulders loosen as soon as her face is covered.

It only takes a few minutes for the truck to roll up the drive to the house. Sarah searches the windows for the figure she'd seen earlier. No one lurks behind the panes. The only silhouette is that of the woods behind the house. Graham had raved about seeing stars up north, but tonight, the sky is overcast. All she can see is dark against dark, the tree-shaped shadows swaying as one, breathing in an irregular rhythm.

Caleb pulls the truck into what looks like a converted carriage house. Inside, it's a normal suburban garage, which Sarah finds reassuring. Power tools hang on a pegboard over a workbench, and a spool of heavy-duty plastic sheeting leans against a chest freezer. Industrial-sized bottles of bleach and boxes of latex gloves are stacked on a shelf. It's no less than what everyone has these days in a pandemic.

She follows Caleb out of the garage, clutching her damp hoodie. Caleb carries her backpack. The house seems bigger now she's standing below its gables, monstrous by Toronto standards, and unnecessarily large for two—now three—people. The woods behind it reach up to the sky. These are the trees from the motel paintings, dark and sinister, moving constantly in the wind.

"Welcome to Sweetside Manor," Caleb announces, his voice droll. He climbs the porch's front steps and holds the door open. "I didn't name the place, by the way. Some ancestor with a taste for grandeur and colonization."

What would that ancestor think of her? She steps warily over the threshold, instinctively afraid of awakening old ghosts. This house must have many.

"No need to be quiet," Caleb says. "Elijah's a night owl. He's probably in his studio or out for a walk."

"At this time of night?"

"It's pretty safe around here."

She raises her eyebrows. He adds, sheepishly, "Well, for us."

Sarah scrapes the borrowed boots on the doormat and pries them off. Standing in the foyer, she's not sure what she'd expected. Ornate Victorian furniture and tarnished chandeliers, to match the house's exterior.

Sweetside Manor is a time capsule, but of about fifty years ago. The space is lined with orange and brown floral wallpaper. Cross-stitched flowers in embroidery hoops follow the rise of a varnished wooden staircase, and a braided rag rug sits below the last step. The air smells like cedar and something oily, like turpentine. Like Elijah's coat.

To Sarah, she might as well have stepped into Victorian times. She's not used to anything older than a generation. She and Graham grew up just north of Toronto, the house freshly built when her parents bought it in the 1990s. Everything that couldn't fit in a suitcase had been left behind in Hong Kong, and even there, the family home was filled with modern flat-pack furniture. And the house where she and Ben rented an apartment is newly renovated, any history exorcised by track lighting and stainless steel appliances. The whitewashed walls were a blank canvas for Ben's moods.

She tries to put her smile into her eyes as she takes in the house. She's fled to the past, instead of the future she'd imagined every time she withdrew just a little more cash from the grocery store ATM to fund her escape.

"I'm afraid it's not classy by Toronto standards," Caleb says, helping her out of the parka and hanging it up in the hall closet. "We were planning to renovate and put the house on Airbnb, but then the pandemic hit."

"It's nice," she lies. "Look, I'm really sorry about the windows. I can help clean up—"

"I'll take care of it in the morning. I'm the one who's sorry. I should've brought you to the house right away. They don't like anyone who's different around here. Even me and Elijah, they treat us like we're outsiders."

He shrugs off his jacket and he is, of course, wearing more plaid beneath it. He seems unaware he's the poster boy for country living, a square-jawed, broad-shouldered mountain man who'd be at home in front of a fire with a couple of hunting dogs.

"I find that hard to believe," Sarah says.

"Mom came from money—the town's named for her family—so they never let us fit in. And after she died, Dad sold off the land she'd owned to a developer who turned it into luxury cottages. They bring in tourist revenue, but everyone's mad we opened the door to more city folks. Shit."

He glances down. There's a smear of blood on the scratched hardwood. "You must've stepped on glass."

Sarah lifts her left foot, revealing a blotch under the toe of her sock. Unbelievable. She broke his motel windows, and now she's bleeding all over this man's home. Karma, perhaps, for what she did to Ben. "I'm sorry about the—"

"For fuck's sake, stop apologizing."

She shuts up, the familiar alarm bell chiming in the back of her head. With his mask on, she can't tell how angry he is. Best to keep smiling and appear harmless and helpless, even though her heart jackrabbits in her chest.

"I'll take a look at your foot upstairs," he says.

Caleb trudges up the stairs with her backpack, and the house springs to life, floorboards groaning under his feet. "Is it only you and your brother here?" Sarah asks, her own footsteps pale echoes of his bold ones as she follows him upstairs.

"Yep. Dad and Grandma and Grandpa Sweet lived here too, until they passed away. Now it's just me and Elijah. This way. You can have the main bedroom. It's got an ensuite bathroom, so you don't have to go into the rest of the house."

Caleb opens a door at the end of the darkened landing. At first, Sarah thinks she's staring at another painting, but then he flicks on the light, and she realizes it's a window looking out on the woods. A king-sized bed sprawls beneath it, next to a well-worn plaid recliner in shades of mustard and taupe. A framed photograph of a man and woman stands on a built-in desk that must have once been a vanity for the lady of the house. From the couple's curling brown hair, Sarah guesses they're Caleb's parents.

The woman is elegant and bird-like in a long wool coat, the fine features of her face weighed down by an unseen sadness. Sarah wonders if she'd been diagnosed with cancer already. The man beside her is all sideburns and shearling and tinted glasses, his large hand weighing down her shoulder. He grins at the camera, proud of his spoils. Sarah shivers. He reminds her of Ben.

Caleb strides forward, driving her further into the room, and motions toward the bed. "Sit. I'll get the first aid kit."

He disappears into the bathroom. Sarah drapes the damp hoodie over her backpack and sinks onto the mattress, anticipation and apprehension scouring her insides.

Caleb emerges with a tube of antiseptic ointment and some gauze. "I can—" she starts, but he waves her off. She peels the sock off her foot, afraid he'll do it himself if she doesn't.

He sits on the recliner and grabs her ankle. She gasps at the sudden heat of his skin. He glances up, brows drawing together. His eyes are as blue as a summer sky, the sky she'd pictured when she'd imagined driving up Highway 11 to her freedom. "Sorry, did I hurt you?"

Sarah shakes her head, unable to speak. He peers at the sole of her foot. A tendril of hair springs over his forehead, and she fights the urge to wind the curl around her fingers. She focuses on her foot instead. Blood smudges the gap beside her big toe. She hadn't felt the cut or noticed the bleeding until it was too late.

Story of her life, again.

"I don't see any broken glass, and it's a small cut. You won't need stitches." He gently dabs some of the ointment on the cut. Sarah hisses at the sting, and the unexpected intimacy of the gesture. "It's all right," he says soothingly.

He wraps clean gauze around her foot and finally releases her. She remembers how to breathe again, taking air through her mouth in shuddering gulps while Caleb returns the supplies to the bathroom. It's been a long time since anyone touched her in kindness, without expecting anything in return.

"Get some sleep. You're safe now," Caleb says. Sarah wants to believe him, but the masculine smell of his deodorant and the crinkle at the corners of his too-blue eyes tell her otherwise. "I'll come by in the morning with breakfast."

"Thank you."

He doesn't turn to leave, his throat constricting below his masked chin like he wants to say something else. They lock gazes for a second too long, until a creak downstairs breaks the silence. Caleb's eyes flit toward the sound, and deep lines appear in his forehead.

"I'd lock your door," he says quietly, and then he's gone.

CHAPTER FOUR

There's no TV or radio in the room, nothing to drown out the wailing of the wind or her own flailing thoughts. The house makes noises, too, keeping her awake with its unfamiliar song. Hardwood squawks, windows creak, radiators clunk and rattle. Footsteps pace nearby, and she can't tell if it's upstairs or downstairs or just outside her door.

When Sarah finally sleeps, it's with the knife under her pillow.

Daylight shining from the room's front windows rouses her in the morning. She thrashes in the strange bed, struggling under the weight of the quilt. Then she remembers she's alone. *Alone, alone, alone.* The word sings in her head along with the wind. Alone save for the two strangers outside her room.

She scrambles out of the bed and plods to the bathroom. The whole house must hear the floorboards warping, the toilet flushing, the pipes grousing. If the brothers have forgotten her presence, she must sound like their father's ghost.

A soft knock sounds on the bedroom door. "Good morning, Sarah," Caleb says. "Would you like breakfast? I can bring you coffee and muffins. Do you have any allergies or dietary needs?"

"Yes, please," she says. "And no, I don't. Thank you."

"How do you take your coffee?"

"Milk and no sugar, please."

She buries the knife at the bottom of her backpack and changes into her clothes. Her pink hoodie is dry, so she puts it on as she's got nothing else warm. At least in daylight, Ben's blood is barely visible.

She tucks the piece of paper with Graham's number on it in her pocket in case she gets the chance to charge her phone. When Caleb's powerful tread rises on the stairs again, she rakes her fingers through her hair in front of the vanity mirror. Thank goodness for the mask to hide her makeup-free face. If only it could hide the dark circles under her eyes from months of restless sleeping.

A knock sounds again. "Room service," Caleb says cheerily.

Sarah smooths down her sweatshirt and opens the door. Caleb breezes in and places a laden tray on the vanity. The scent of coffee and aftershave is intoxicating, and she wonders if Caleb's cheeks are smooth under the mask today.

"Are you sure I can't at least pay you for the food?" Sarah says.

"Don't worry about it. I bet you don't eat half of what Elijah does. Hang on a sec."

He slips out of the room and returns with a stack of books, setting them on the vanity beside the tray. "Not sure if these are your thing, but you said you were a writer. I'm afraid it's all we have in way of entertainment. We don't have wifi and the only TV is downstairs." He shrugs apologetically. "There was never any point in getting internet up here when we spent all our waking hours at the motel."

Sarah crosses to the vanity and inspects the spines. *Bulfinch's Mythology. Jane Eyre. Heart of Darkness. Macbeth. The Tempest.* She opens the front cover of *Bulfinch's* and reads *Jacob Vass* incised on the flyleaf in stark black ink. Another white man with a Biblical name. Although she supposes her name's from the Bible, too.

She must have frowned because Caleb's eyes crinkle. "I bet you're wondering why a small-town hick like me has these. Mom taught high school English, and Dad had a thing for ancient Greece. And yes, I actually have read—Hold on."

Caleb pulls a vibrating cell phone from the back pocket of his jeans. "Hi, Uncle Isaac. Yeah, I brought her up to the house. I put her in Dad's room. We'll be safe."

Safe from the vandals or safe from her? Sarah shapes her face into a pleasant expression, so he can see she's not a threat.

"What's that? Fuck. Okay. I'll be there as soon as I can."

He tucks the phone back into his jeans. "Shit. Kaylee Brighton's been spotted at the drugstore. She's supposed to stay home since she snuck off to a clandestine party in Huntsville last week. I have to help Uncle Isaac reinforce her quarantine."

Sarah remembers the plywood in the back of his truck, and she suddenly doesn't feel like eating.

"I'll be back by lunchtime. Do you eat burgers? Sal's in town has the best bacon cheeseburgers. I can grab us takeout."

"Sure." It sounds good, but it's not like she has much choice.

"Great." His eyes sparkle above his mask as if they've just made a date, and Sarah's stomach warms.

Until he adds, "Lock the door and don't leave the room," and she remembers why she's really here. Her skin crawls as she imagines him hammering plywood across the doorframe, the brute strength of his arms driving in the nails one by one.

When she stands in the front window, picking at a muffin and watching the truck drive away, she realizes she forgot to ask him for a phone charger.

The wind surges, battering against the windows like a bird fighting its reflection. Sarah picks up *The Tempest* and the mug of coffee and sinks into the recliner. Caleb's mother has written *Meredith Vass* on the inside cover in the neat handwriting Sarah would expect from a teacher. The name suits the delicate woman in the photo on the vanity. Sarah flips the page to Act 1. She doesn't need the CliffsNotes to know she's Ferdinand, washed up on this unexpected island.

As she turns the pages, she smells tobacco, so faint she's not sure she's imagining it. The sickly sweet scent pricks her nose and sends the hairs on her arms rising. She squirms in the chair, the air suddenly sucked out of the room like it did every time Ben entered. Her lungs strain to breathe, her senses convinced someone is looming behind her. Caleb's father, reading over her shoulder.

She tosses the book on the bed and springs out of the recliner, heart racing.

She's alone, save for the shrieking wind. The house, though, is silent. Caleb's brother, Elijah, must be asleep. No ghosts stirring, except for the ones in her head.

Rattled and reluctant to sit any longer, she unlocks the door.

She can't be carrying the virus. Since the start of the pandemic, she's barely interacted with anyone other than Ben. It's been months, and neither she nor Ben have even gotten a cold. She'll just have a quick look for a phone charger. Caleb has a cell, so there must be one lying around.

She won't rifle through papers or open any drawers, nothing that would violate his privacy. If she doesn't see one, she'll return to her room like a good girl, and no one will be the wiser.

Sarah puts on her mask, slips her dead phone into her pocket, and steps into the hallway with her half-empty coffee mug. If anyone catches her outside her room, she can say she was hoping for a refill.

There are two doors ahead, one closed and one open. Elijah must be sleeping behind the closed door. She doesn't want to wake him; she'll have to peek into Caleb's room another time. She's afraid to, anyway, in case she finds something that'll make her dislike him, like a stack of porn magazines or the same World War II history books Ben owned.

She tiptoes down the stairs, breath straining behind her mask with the effort to keep quiet, and finds the kitchen. It's as outdated as the rest of the house. Rustic wooden cabinets, brown patterned linoleum, a backsplash of orange and white tiles. Sarah almost laughs out loud at the beige rotary phone hanging on the floral wallpaper. She picks up the receiver, but remembers Graham's cell still has a Toronto area code. She reluctantly puts it back. Nice girls don't make long-distance calls without asking, and being nice is how she's survived this far.

She locates the coffeemaker, the carafe blessedly half full and the heating element powered on. She refills her mug and then locates the milk. The fridge holds mostly convenience foods that can be eaten by hand. Baby carrots, cold cuts, a grocery store rotisserie chicken, a leftover slice of pizza on a plastic-wrapped plate. Sarah smirks. A bachelor fridge.

No phone charger plugged into the outlet with the coffeemaker, however, or lying out on the table or laminate countertops.

She splashes milk in her coffee and slips off her mask to drink. Sipping carefully, she wanders into the dining room, where a grandfather clock loudly echoes her fraught heartbeat. The bite of furniture polish and tobacco lingers in the air. She checks behind her shoulder for Caleb's father again, but sees no one.

A bulky teak dining set squats in the middle of the room. On one side, a matching hutch is stacked with books instead of the good china, mostly faded classics like the ones in her room and a few textbooks on hospitality management. A cluster of framed photos face the hutch on the opposite wall. Meredith Vass holding a baby on her lap. A grim-faced elderly white couple. A pair of chestnut-haired boys standing in front of a Christmas tree, the older a lanky adolescent, the younger a chubby-cheeked toddler. Next to them, in another photo, Jacob Vass lounges in the plaid recliner, a pipe jutting from one broad fist—identical to Caleb's fists, Sarah notes—laughing so heartily the camera reveals the metal crowns at the back of his mouth. Meredith perches on the arm of the recliner, hands crossed demurely, her own smile tight and close-mouthed. The smiles of the dead.

Sarah turns away from Caleb's family and crosses the foyer to the front room. It's granny chic meets hunting lodge: wood paneling, floral upholstery encased in plastic slipcovers, and a stag's head mounted on a wall. Surprisingly the room doesn't smell the way it looks; it smells faintly of bleach, like the motel.

She clutches the coffee mug for warmth, unnerved by all the relics of the past. She's not used to living in a home with so much history. The scratches on the dining table, the shiny spots on the staircase banister, the scuffs on the floorboards all betray previous inhabitants. She's afraid to stray onto the front room's vinyl floor runners for fear Grandma Sweet will appear and scold her for drinking out of an open cup around the good furniture. Heaven knows this house has the space for ghosts, and anyway, there's nowhere else for them to go in this remote location.

Sarah continues her creeping to the back of the house and finds a den. It appears a typical bachelor sanctum, leather sofa pushed aside to make room for a weight bench and treadmill in front of a large-screen TV. But a chill travels across the back of her neck and stirs her hair. She hears a crashing like ocean waves, and for once, it's not the blood in her ears.

The glass sliding door that should look out on the backyard is slightly ajar and covered in yellowing newspaper on the outside. A corner of the newspaper lifts and rattles, and she smells the cedar and turpentine scent of Elijah's parka. Curiosity gets the better of her, despite her pounding heart. She slides the glass door open, revealing a large painting on an easel.

But that's not what holds Sarah's attention. The wall ahead is made of plastic sheeting, thundering under the wind's fists and rippling like the choppy surface of a lake. Through the semi-transparent plastic, the woods are twisted shadows. Like in the paintings at the motel, and on the easel's canvas.

Similar canvases are propped to the left and right, against the room's glass sides. An old dresser serves as a makeshift palette, its top mottled by blobs of paint. A handful of brushes sits in a coffee can on a folding table littered with paint tubes, gnarled twigs, and a small animal skull. A shearling coat hangs over the arm of a loveseat, twin to the recliner in the main bedroom.

Sarah recognizes the coat from the photo of Caleb's father upstairs. Is this Jacob Vass's studio? His hands—Caleb's hands—would be capable of the furious brushstrokes.

"Dad was putting in a sunroom," says a voice from behind her, "but he never got the chance to finish it."

Sarah spins around, splashing coffee over her hand. A young man in his twenties stands in the doorway. He's shorter and leaner than Caleb, and his eyes brown instead of blue, but he shares his brother's wayward chestnut hair and easy posture. He's not wearing a mask, revealing softer-edged cheekbones and a sloping nose, as if a sculptor had started to chisel Caleb's face but gave up. His mouth is thin, stubborn, and a little sad.

"You must be Sarah," the man with Meredith Vass's mouth says.

A roar sounds in Sarah's ears, and it's not the plastic billowing in the sunroom's paneless windows. "You shouldn't be down here," the man says. Like Caleb, he has a forehead that frowns too much.

She wipes her wet hands on her jeans and offers a contrite smile. "I'm sorry, I got restless."

The drooping line of his mouth turns up, and he transforms. He's not as handsome as Caleb, but his manner is sweet and boyish. The roar in Sarah's ears hushes. The guileless pleasure on his face instantly puts her at ease. "It can be our secret. I'm Elijah, by the way. Caleb's brother."

"I figured. Nice to meet you, Elijah."

"Do you like my paintings?"

"These are yours?" She notices the smudges on his hands, the fingernails stained near-black. "I do. I saw them back at the motel. They're very good."

Elijah beams like a golden retriever with a newly fetched stick. "Thank you. Do you know where Caleb went?"

"Um, he said Kaylee Brighton's been spotted at a drugstore?"

"Uncle Isaac called him in, huh? Okay, we've got some time. Want a tour of the house?"

Hope flares behind Sarah's sternum. Elijah seems eager to please, and most importantly, happy to bend Caleb's rules. "I'm actually looking for a phone charger. Do you have one?"

"I don't have a cell. I can help you find Caleb's, though."

"Great. I checked downstairs already, but not upstairs. I didn't want to nose around the bedrooms."

She fishes her mask out of her pocket and slips it back on. Elijah steps out of the doorway and lets her through. He slides the door behind her, shutting off the sound of struggling plastic.

He lopes away from the sunroom, and she has to jog to catch up. "Did you see our parlor?" he says.

She assumes he means the front room. "Yes, it's very nice," she says automatically.

"Don't lie, it's hideous. Grandma put down the plastic before I was born. Dad never took it off, and Caleb never got around to it either."

"It's very practical." A preventative measure, to deter future generations from leaving their mark. No new ghosts allowed in Sweetside Manor, at least in that room.

"You're a good liar," he says cheerfully, and Sarah's not sure if she should be offended or pleased. "Dad shot that buck," he adds, as they pass the parlor's doorway.

"Do you hunt too?" Her hands tighten around the mug with the effort to keep her tone affable. It's one thing to be trapped with two strange men; it's another to be trapped with two strange men and a gun.

"Gosh, no." Elijah looks shocked she'd even ask. He leads her up the stairs, each step crying a protest. "I found those antlers, though. It's interesting what you can find in the woods. Caleb shot a rabbit once when we were kids, but cried after. Dad wasn't happy about that."

Sarah likes the Vass brothers a little more and their father a little less. Elijah shows her a succession of cold, empty rooms, lined with faded wallpaper and carpet, and a steep back staircase he explains was meant for servants. In the manor's heyday, Sarah probably would've only been allowed on those stairs. "Grandma and Grandpa lived in that room," he says, pointing to a large room at the end of the hall, "but the rest have been empty for a while. I think Dad was hoping Caleb would get married and fill them with kids."

"Caleb never married?" Sarah asks, trying to sound casual.

"He's had a few girlfriends, but nothing serious. Why, do you like him?"

She's glad she put on her mask so he can't see her burning cheeks. "He's been very kind."

"Caleb's always been kind. But—" His mouth thins, and he looks like his mother again. "I'd be careful around him. He hasn't been the same since Dad died."

The flush across Sarah's skin chills. Elijah adds, "Everyone in this house ends up dying. Grandma, Grandpa, Mom. I was too young, but Caleb would've had to watch them die. Have you ever watched anyone die?"

He cocks his head at her, genuinely curious. She pushes her mask down and takes a sip of coffee to wet her suddenly dry throat. "Not that I know of," she says jokingly. She's a good liar, after all.

"The charger must be in Caleb's room. Come on." Elijah spins on his heel, and she follows, dizzy from the sudden change in conversation. It's probably been a long time since he's talked to anyone other than Caleb.

Elijah barges through the door to his brother's room. Sarah hangs back in the doorway. To her relief, there's nothing embarrassing on display. Clothes slung over a chair. A heavy dresser with brass drawer pulls. A clock radio and a paperback copy of *Of Mice and Men* on a nightstand. Navy blue sheets neatly smoothed over the queen-sized bed. The effect is anonymous and neutral, like out of a furniture catalog. No photographs or artwork, but who needs them when the open curtains frame the wild landscape outside?

"He sometimes charges his phone there," Elijah says, motioning to the nightstand. He opens the drawer and rummages around. "Aha!"

He holds up a cable. Sarah's stomach sinks. "It's the wrong kind. I've got a—an older model." She thinks regretfully of her old phone, sitting at the bottom of the highway rest stop trash can, completely wiped and the SIM card flushed down the toilet at home. She didn't want to leave it behind at the apartment. It could be construed as evidence of premeditation, when she'd meant to slip out without Ben's notice.

"I'm sorry I wasn't able to help." He tucks the cable back into the drawer, his mouth drooping.

"It's all right, I appreciate you looking. You and Caleb have already done so much for me."

"It's no trouble. We always keep clean sheets on Dad's bed in case he comes back."

"Comes back from where?" She thought he and Caleb had said he was dead. Her skin crawls at the thought of the sickly tobacco scent and powerful hands. She wouldn't want Jacob Vass to return unexpectedly, like Papa Bear growling, *Someone's been sleeping in my bed.*

"The woods. That's where they all go."

Do you hear them? Sarah swallows, and her pulse thrums a warning. "Why did you ask if I heard screaming when I called the house last night?"

"Because they all did. Before they—" Elijah's eyes widen at the sudden crunch of tires on salted pavement. His hand shoots out to grab her sleeve, the knuckles white under the paint stains. She startles at the urgent touch. "Caleb's coming. Go to your room. If he finds you out here—"

Sarah's chest squeezes, more alarmed by the terror lighting up Elijah's face than the ominous growl of the truck pulling into the garage. Elijah releases her sleeve, already running down the landing. "I'd lock your door."

"What?"

But it's too late. Elijah has disappeared down the stairs like a ghost.

CHAPTER FIVE

Sarah dashes to her room and locks the door. Ripping off her mask, she hurriedly sets the coffee mug on the tray and then flops onto the recliner. She opens *The Tempest* but doesn't read, only listens for Caleb above the racing of her heart.

Why would Elijah warn her to lock her door? Why would Caleb say the same thing? What are they not telling her about the other? Unless Jacob Vass is actually out in the woods and due to come home any day now.

Caleb's solid gait sends the stairs grumbling. "Elijah, were you in my room again?" he calls out, his voice sharp as a knife. Sarah's pulse jitters. Caleb has been kind, but how well does she really know him? *He hasn't been the same since Dad died.*

Ben had been kind to her, too, at first.

Elijah's reply drifts from downstairs. "I was looking for Bulfinch's."

"I gave it to Sarah. What did I tell you?"

"I know, I just wanted to look something up. Sorry."

"Don't do it again," Caleb growls, and it's like a completely different man is speaking. The voice belongs to the heavy-handed man in the family photos, not the boy who cried after shooting a rabbit.

When the knock finally comes, she jumps. "Sarah? Can I come in?" Caleb asks.

Sarah gets up and opens the door. The brass knob is tarnished, marked by Jacob and Meredith Vass's hands. Another scar left on the house's body to remember its ghosts by.

Caleb strides in. Sarah backs away and perches back on the recliner. His eyes crinkle above his mask, the perfect host once more. Maybe she'd imagined his angry outburst, and Elijah's look of terror when they heard the truck pulling up. Or maybe she's projecting too much on a normal sibling relationship. How many times have she and Graham bickered viciously over a trivial issue?

Still, she pushes her face into a pleasant, unthreatening shape. "Hi, Caleb. Did everything go okay with Kaylee Brighton?"

"She didn't put up a fuss, thank God. It's not like we leave people to starve, but sometimes they get really pissed off. Old Man Doherty waved a hunting rifle at Uncle Isaac last month. Uncle Isaac could've shot him, and everyone would've said he'd done the right thing."

He shakes his head. Sarah holds her smile although the spot between her shoulder blades itches.

"How's the foot?" he asks.

"It's fine."

"Can I see?"

She nods. Caleb sinks onto the bed and takes her foot in his hands. His fingers burn against her skin as he rolls off her sock, and she has to remind herself to breathe. Elijah can't be scared of someone with hands as gentle as this.

"Looks like it started bleeding again, but it's okay. Were you moving around a lot?"

She laughs nervously. "I was feeling cooped up."

"How about I take you outside for a walk? It's stopped snowing. We can eat our burgers."

"I'd like that," she says, and means it.

"Great. Meet you downstairs in ten."

He whisks her tray away. She pulls her sock back on, feeling disappointed. The touch of her own fingers is not the same as his.

She puts on her mask and finds Caleb in the kitchen, rustling through a paper takeout bag. He gives her a heavy foil-wrapped burger that takes both hands to hold.

"I can't eat all of this. Can I cut it in half?" she asks.

"All the knives are in the dishwasher. I'm afraid you'll just have to deal with it."

There's a third burger in the bag, which he leaves on the table. For

Elijah, she guesses. She hasn't seen or heard him since she got downstairs. Caleb holds her burger while she laces up the boots and puts on the parka. Now that she's met Elijah, the cedar and turpentine scent is comforting, like an old blanket.

Outside, the sky is a muted grey, choked with low-hanging clouds. To Sarah, it feels like a ceiling pressing her into the ground. Every day, every hour, the space she occupies shrinks. It's like those last months of lockdown with Ben. His resentment and restlessness had ballooned as he lost yet another job while she continued to work, forcing her to make herself as small as possible.

At the bottom of the porch steps, Caleb takes off his mask and inhales deeply. Sarah takes that as permission to remove her own mask. He turns to her and smiles. He's shaved. She wants to think it's for her.

She takes a deep breath as well. The air has a crispness to it, like biting into an apple, but it's not frigid enough to prick the inside of her nose. Graham had said winter was different up north. The temperatures plummeted lower, yes, but it's a dry cold, not the damp from Lake Ontario that burrows under your skin and into your bones. She can almost understand why he took that job in Timmins.

The long shape of the Suicide Motel crouches in the distance, its roof blanched white from the blizzard. Sarah can't see the broken glass the vandals left behind, but she knows it's under the carpet of snow. Such is winter, good at hiding ugly truths. Beyond the motel, the grey ribbon of Highway 11 unfurls into the horizon. It's far enough away that she can't hear the trucks grinding by. She can't hear anything, only her ragged breath and her boots crunching on the driveway.

She follows Caleb to the back of the house. The woods that hug the property stand impossibly tall, their top branches shaggy as waterlogged feathers with the weight of the snow. It hurts Sarah's neck to look up at them. A path trampled between the trees weaves into shadow. She wonders who carved that path, Caleb or Elijah. Elijah, she decides. It explains the souvenirs of the woods in his studio.

"I can't imagine growing up with a forest in my backyard," Sarah says, because there's nothing complimentary she can say about this ragged landscape. She wouldn't have wanted to play in *these* woods if they were behind her parents' home. She would've wanted a pretty forest out of a fairy tale, with lush green leaves and a sky the color of Caleb's eyes. Not skeletal trees clustered together for warmth, the base of their trunks naked and prickly from lack of sun.

"We were lucky to grow up here. I liked living in Toronto when I was in college, but I missed the outdoors."

Sarah wraps her arms around herself. "I prefer the city."

"Really? Our hefty tourist population begs to differ."

Her mouth twists. "I didn't grow up going to the cottage on weekends. *My* family doesn't have lakeside property that Grandpa bought in the 50s for a song."

He smiles apologetically. "Fair enough."

"It's nice to visit, but I don't feel safe."

"What're you talking about? It's totally safe."

And here it is, the conversation she's had with Ben and past boyfriends, and even white girlfriends, who are always mystified that she prefers the city's bustling anonymity. She's tired of explaining how she feels and being told she's wrong. Instead, she says, "I don't like that no one can hear you scream."

Caleb grins. "Well, if you scream in Toronto, they'll hear you, but no one cares."

Sarah can't help laughing, because it's true.

"It's safe as houses here. Well, maybe not this house." He gestures toward the swelling plastic tacked onto the end of the unfinished sunroom. A shadowy figure stands on the other side, but when Sarah blinks, it's gone.

"Dad was in the middle of building a sunroom before he died. I didn't have time to put in the back windows before the first snowfall, so I put up the plastic. Elijah turned it into a studio, and it's been that way ever since. He's very talented. You've seen his paintings?"

"Paintings?" she says, playing dumb. He can't know she's been in the studio.

"The ones in the motel. The dark trees."

"Oh! Yes, they're very good. Does he exhibit anywhere?"

"Just the motel." Caleb shakes his head sadly. "He's much too sensitive for the outside world."

A picnic table stands in the clearing before the woods. Caleb brushes the snow off the bench and sits down, gesturing that Sarah should join him. She sits on the opposite end, grateful to have the pandemic as an excuse to not sit too close.

She peels back the foil and bites into the burger. It's thick and juicy, and she pushes back her sleeves to avoid dripping on the cuffs of Elijah's parka.

Caleb stiffens.

Sarah follows his gaze to her left wrist. Bruises circle the pale skin like a bracelet, fresh and purple. With all the layers she has on for winter, she hadn't known they'd been forming, like a message in invisible ink come to light.

"Do you want to tell me about them?" Caleb says.

Sarah pastes on her best smile. "Oh, that's nothing. I must've banged it on something."

"Bullshit."

Sarah's scalp prickles at the fury in his voice. "No, it's okay. It wasn't my—wasn't a boyfriend." She wants charming Caleb back, not angry Caleb. It *was* okay, anyway. It was the only time Ben ever hurt her. Physically. He'd come out of the shower sooner than he should have and caught her in the kitchen, jamming a water bottle in her full backpack.

"It's not. I recognize that kind of bruise. I used to have a matching set myself from my dad. He'd drink too much and fly into these rages."

At her surprised blink, he smiles faintly. "I know. I look like I can hold my own in a fight. I started lifting weights when I was a teen so I could hit back. The irony is, I earned Dad's respect by becoming a 'man.' Whatever that means."

Sarah remembers the skinny boy in the Christmas photo, and her heart goes out to him. "Did he stop when you—?"

"Yeah. At least, I thought he was done. I thought it would be safe to go away to college, but Elijah—"

She thinks of Elijah's sad face, the mirror of his mother's. His enthusiastic grin, so eager to please because people might turn on you otherwise. She knows what it's like.

The pieces fall into place, and a heavy sadness blankets her stomach. "You came back for Elijah. I'm so sorry."

"You really like apologizing for things that aren't your fault, don't you?"

He has no idea.

"Don't be sorry," he says. "We're still here, and that asshole isn't. I'm not going to lie; neither of us were sad when he disappeared. Even if it did make our reputation worse in this town." Caleb jerks his head in the direction of the motel. "You must've heard Jerry call it the Suicide Motel. In the past ten years, two other men stopped at the motel and were never seen again, and now we're the local urban legend. Joseph Singh got caught in a blizzard on his way to Sudbury, and Stuart McGee was heading to Toronto for a conference. They never found them. Hike about an hour east, and there's a lake. Keep walking long enough through these woods, and you'll end up in Algonquin Park. So many ways you could vanish in the backcountry."

Sarah swallows, the burger suddenly a greasy lump in her throat. "Not the work of a serial killer?" And he'd said it was safe here.

Caleb chuckles. "You've been watching too much TV. Joseph Singh and Stuart McGee were like Dad. Angry men who had a lot of issues. Their families were all unsurprised. Relieved, even. Uncle Isaac figures they wanted to vanish for good. He never found any signs of struggle."

If you wanted to disappear, this would be the place to do it. Sarah imagines the treetops closing over her head, swaddling her. Keeping her safe at last, with the men who'd also sought sanctuary. *Do you hear them?*

She shivers, despite her down-filled coat. "What did Elijah mean, when I called last night? He asked if I heard screaming."

Caleb smiles ruefully. "That's part of the legend. Elijah worked the night shift at the motel. The men who disappeared—they both called in the middle of the night, complaining they could hear screaming in the woods. It was just the wind and their mental state, but now everyone says this place drives people mad. You've heard the way the wind goes through the trees? It's creepy if you're not prepared for it."

He gazes wistfully at the pines, and she wishes she could see what he sees. "It's beautiful but lonely. I suppose I could sell everything and move, but Elijah adores the woods, and I have to take care of him. I'm the only one who really understands him. You have a brother, right? You said you were on your way to see him."

"Yes. Actually, I was hoping to call him but my phone's dead. Do you have a charger?" She reaches inside her coat for the phone.

Caleb inspects the socket. "Mm, sorry. Mine's different, and Elijah doesn't have a phone."

"Could you ask the mechanic to get mine out of my car?"

Caleb grimaces and puts down the burger. "Shit. I was hoping to break it to you gently. Lars is sick, so the garage is closed, and his staff are in quarantine, too. You won't be getting your car back for a while."

Despair sinks its claws into Sarah's stomach. She's already stayed here long enough. "Could you get me a charger in town?"

"Most people drive up to North Bay for stuff like that. We've got groceries and hardware, and ice cream for summer tourists, but not much else. I'd ask around if I could borrow one, but—" His eyebrows steeple in an apology. Considering no one wants to even touch her car, no one is going to lend her a thing. "Is your brother going to be worried? I could ask Uncle Isaac to—"

"No." No, Graham wasn't expecting her, and no, she doesn't want the police to talk to him before she does. "Could I use your phone? I'm afraid it's long distance, he just moved and still has a Toronto cell number. He could drive down and get me, and I could pick up my car later."

Caleb shakes his head. "I don't think that's a good idea. You should finish your quarantine first. The garage will be open shortly after."

Sarah's throat closes up, and the inside of her mouth suddenly tastes rancid. "I don't have the virus. I barely saw anyone in Toronto."

"I believe you. You don't seem like the type of girl who breaks rules."

It's a small triumph. The mask she's had to put on since yesterday morning—since the beginning of lockdown—is working. Let Caleb think she's a nice girl. Nice girls don't walk out on their boyfriends. Nice girls don't keep knives at the bottom of their backpacks.

"I'm not worried about you spreading the virus. But what Uncle Isaac says, goes."

Sarah impulsively squeezes Caleb's arm, as if she can make him feel the weight of her urgency through his coat sleeve. His jaw twitches. She wonders how long it's been since someone other than his brother has touched him. "I don't want to impose on your hospitality." It's what a nice girl would say.

"It's not an imposition. I like having someone else around besides Elijah." He smiles, and her breathing quickens, fueled by anxiety and longing. "Don't worry, Sarah. You're safe here. From *everything*," he adds, glancing at her wrist again.

He crumples up the foil from his burger. Sarah reluctantly withdraws her hand from his arm and wraps up the remains of hers. She rises from the picnic table, the food sitting in her stomach like a rock, and follows Caleb back around the house. At first she thinks their footsteps are echoing in the silence, but then Caleb turns. "Oh, there's Elijah," he says. A hunched figure in a shearling coat crosses the backyard, heading toward the woods.

Caleb calls his brother's name. Elijah glances up. "Elijah, this is Sarah."

Sarah lifts a hand in greeting, careful to keep her face neutral. The mask again. Elijah's face splits in the grin she knows well now, and he waves back. "Nice to meet you, Sarah!" he calls back. Then he disappears down the trampled path into the woods. The trees seem to close in over him, hiding he'd ever existed.

Caleb pauses, as if weighing his thoughts. "Be careful around him," he says, quietly. "He hasn't been the same since Dad died."

"He—" Sarah stops, catching herself. *He said the same thing about you.*

The planes of Caleb's face may as well be chiseled from stone. "Let's go in."

CHAPTER SIX

Sarah sleeps restlessly that night. The wind outside the windows scrapes its nails against the glass, calling her into the woods. It promises the woods will keep her safe. No one will be able to find her there. The pines will enshroud her like they did Jacob Vass and the other men.

She jolts awake, heart pounding, wondering if the woods drove those men mad or if they were mad in the first place. *Alone, alone, alone,* the wind sings. Or maybe the song is coming from inside her head. It doesn't matter.

The wind howls its agreement.

In the morning, Caleb drops off breakfast and takes away the dinner dishes. He's in a rush, meeting Sarah's eyes fleetingly. She wants to reach out and touch him again, but doesn't. "I need to go back to the motel," he says brusquely. "Elijah will bring your lunch."

He hasn't glanced at her bruises again, but that's fine. It's easier to let him think Ben had always been rough. She doesn't want to tell him what really happened, because she's afraid he won't be so kind anymore.

And so she sits at the vanity and sips her coffee, disappointed he didn't ask to re-bandage her foot. She also wishes she'd asked him for a radio. Something to drown out her thoughts and her thudding heartbeat. The wind and the house and Jacob Vass's ghost are her only company. Caleb's father leers up at her from the framed photograph. *Join me,* he seems to say, his hand curled over his wife's shoulder. Sarah smells stale tobacco and knocks the frame face down, shoulders heaving. It's the scent of the coffee, she tells herself. But there's no avoiding the discolored doorknobs, or the pockmarked headboard and hardwood floor, or the threadbare seat of the recliner. All souvenirs of an angry, violent man.

She understands why neither Caleb nor Elijah have moved into this room. *We always put clean sheets on the bed in case Dad comes back.* Ten years is a long time for a man to be missing, presumed dead. But can Jacob Vass really be gone when he's shaped so much of who they are?

How long will Ben keep his residence in her head? Will she keep the metaphorical sheets on his bed in case he comes back?

No. He can't come back. It's over. It ended in their apartment kitchen as soon as the knife had touched him.

But Jacob Vass's story ended in the lonely, hungry woods, and his sons still keep a room for him.

Snow whirls around the window, and in the distance, the boughs beckon. The glass is sealed with plastic film in the annual Canadian tradition of weatherizing old windows. Sarah thinks of the parlor with its vinyl runners and the layers of plastic cocooning Elijah's studio. It's as if Sweetside Manor is hermetically sealed. A bubble to keep its inhabitants in and—

And *what* out?

She picks up *Macbeth* and settles into the recliner. It's a day for witches and prophecies. The trees peek through the window above the bed. Malcolm's living forest, marching ever closer.

A knock sounds as Lady Macbeth is scrubbing her hands. "Hi, Sarah," Elijah says outside. "Caleb told me to leave your lunch by the door, but do you want to come downstairs instead?"

Sarah jumps at the chance for a change of scenery. "Sure. Just give me a minute."

Be careful around him. She can't believe there's anything to fear from Elijah, with his sweet, sad face. But she digs the washcloth-wrapped knife out of her backpack and tucks it into the kangaroo pocket of her hoodie.

She unlocks the door. Elijah grins, happy to see her. The sleeves of his sweater are a little too long, making him look like a schoolboy. She immediately feels foolish for bringing the knife. Caleb had probably meant she should be extra kind to him. Of course, neither brother would be the same after their father's death. The death of a close family member —who was also an abuser—would dredge up conflicting emotions. They're as wounded as she is.

"How long have you been up?" Sarah asks as Elijah leads her down the stairs.

"Since about eleven. I'm usually in bed by four or five. I don't need to stay up now that the motel's closed, but I like it when it's quiet. I try to listen for the screams the men heard."

Another person might think he was joking. "And have you heard them?" Because she thinks *she* has.

His face falls. "No. Not yet."

In the kitchen, a loaf of bread and a bundle of cold cuts sprawl on the counter next to a tub of pre-washed lettuce, a jar of pickles, and another of mayonnaise. Elijah hands her one of two plates, but she takes both of them. "Here, I'll make yours too. It's the least I can do for eating your food," she says.

She understands why Caleb stays when Elijah rewards her with a brilliant smile. Someone this ingenuous needs protecting. She washes her hands and looks around for a knife to spread the mayonnaise. "There," Elijah says, pointing to the drawer closest to the fridge.

She pulls the drawer open and peers down at the empty slot in the silverware tray. Remembering what Caleb said the previous day, she checks the dishwasher. The basket only holds a pair of coffee spoons.

"Are you looking for a knife? He's not supposed to have knives," Elijah says.

The back of Sarah's neck prickles. "You mean Caleb?"

"I threw them all away after Dad died. He fits the profile of those who disappeared from the motel. Big men who don't talk about their feelings. He's so much like Dad."

Sarah swallows hard, conscious of the weight of the knife against her belly. How else is Caleb like his father? Elijah says, "Oh, he's told you. Don't worry, he'd never hurt me, but it's like he—he's got a storm inside him."

Don't they all, a voice in the back of Sarah's head says.

"I was afraid he'd hurt himself," Elijah adds.

Who's taking care of whom? Sarah almost laughs out loud. The only knife in the house is the one in her pocket. It explains all the convenience foods in the fridge.

She grabs a spoon from the drawer and spreads the mayo on the bread with the back of it. Elijah seats himself at the table. She sets down the sandwiches and takes the seat opposite him, startling when he reaches across the table and clasps her hand in his. His cold fingers twine around hers, and she relaxes, touched he would seek human connection with her. "Let us give thanks."

"To whom?" She hasn't seen any signs of religion in the house except for *Bulfinch's Mythology*.

"The woods, of course."

She should've known from the paintings that the woods are Elijah's god. A merciless Old Testament god who demands devotion and sacrifice, but a god nonetheless. Elijah bows his head. She follows suit, silently thanking the woods for hiding her.

Elijah releases her hand. "Any luck with the phone charger?"

"No. Caleb said he wouldn't be able to get one in town." She slumps at the table, shoulders rising to her ears under the weight of her despondency. "I need to call my brother. Graham could come get me, and I'd be out of your hair."

"Is he older or younger?"

"Older."

"Like Caleb."

Sarah rolls her eyes. "Yes. The older one, the responsible one. I'm worried about him, though. He and his wife split up earlier this year, and then he took a teaching job at a college as far away as possible. I don't think he's taken the change well. Though it's hard to say."

"You're not close?"

"No, he's pretty tight-lipped about his feelings."

"Exactly like Caleb." Elijah gestures to the phone hanging on the wall. "Go ahead, you can call him."

Hope lightens the weight on her shoulders, but her instinct is to still play nice. "It's long distance. I only have his cell and it's a Toronto number."

"That's okay, I'm sure it's not expensive."

"But Caleb said—"

"It's my phone too."

Sarah shoots him a grateful look. She puts down her sandwich and gets up from the table. The piece of paper with Graham's number is in her back pocket. She pulls it out and picks up the receiver, scowling at the rotary dial. "Is this the only phone in the house?" She doesn't remember seeing one in the other rooms.

"Uh-huh. Caleb's got a cell, and no one ever wants to talk to me."

It takes forever to dial eleven digits. Sarah taps her foot restlessly as Graham's phone begins to ring. Too late, she realizes if he doesn't recognize the number, he might not pick up. She can always leave a message—but what can she say? How can she sum up the past few days—and months—in thirty seconds?

To her relief, Graham answers. "Graham Ng speaking," he says.

"Graham!" she blurts out.

"Sarah? Where are you calling from? That's not a Toronto area code."

"I know. I'm in Sweetside. It's a little town about a couple hours north of Toronto."

"What the hell are you doing there? Is Ben with you?"

Her knuckles whiten around the receiver. "No. Listen, I need your help. I was coming to see you, and my car broke down, and it's going to be a while before it gets fixed."

"Why don't you call Ben?"

"I left him." She doesn't say where or how she left him.

Graham's slow exhalation rattles in her ear. "What'd you do that for?"

She twists the phone cord around her fingers. "It was a long time coming," she says weakly.

"Jesus, you've been together for what—eight years now? Did you go to relationship counseling?"

"No. He—he's not a good person, Graham. Counseling wouldn't have helped."

"What, did he hit you?"

She closes her eyes briefly. "Well, no."

Graham's breath rattles again. Sarah adds, aware of Elijah's curious eyes on her, "He was cheating on me."

"He'd never do that. Do you have any proof?"

"No, but it was obvious. He was always texting someone, and he wouldn't tell me who it was." And then there were the little things before the pandemic, which she can't explain to Graham because he won't take her seriously. The sudden whiff of another person's perfume, like the pipe tobacco that haunts Jacob Vass's bedroom. Or coming home to find the curtains drawn, and the bedroom closet and dresser drawers all neatly shut when normally they'd be a little ajar. By themselves, the little things might mean nothing, but together, they painted a bigger picture.

"But you don't have any proof." Graham sighs exasperatedly. "Take it from me. You don't throw away so many years together on a whim. Did you at least talk to him about it?"

"Yes. He denied it, of course." And stormed out to sleep on the sofa, and she found herself apologizing because his anger took up all the air in the room, and she was suffocating. Lockdown had stirred his mercurial moods into even more of a hornet's nest, because he couldn't get out to see this other woman, couldn't leave Sarah because he was broke and unemployed and thought himself above living with his mother. And she couldn't kick him out because he'd rage and play the victim, and she was terrified all that fury would spill over into physical violence.

Like it had when she'd tried to leave.

"But he's a liar, Graham. He lies all the time about things. Money, his smoking—" Lies she could never prove, and he sure as hell would never admit. It had been maddening to exist in two opposing realities at once, like Schrödinger's cat.

"And you've never told him white lies? Everyone lies in a relationship," Graham says, and Sarah thinks viciously that maybe Angie was right to divorce him.

"He lies so you don't get mad," he adds, and her teeth grind together because that's what *he* always said. "I'm sure it's a misunderstanding."

"It's *abuse*," she snaps, and the familiar roar surges in her ears as her body anticipates the blowback. First he'll deny it. Then he'll lash out. If his anger doesn't cow her, he'll turn on a dime and pin the blame on her. Even though Graham isn't Ben, at this moment, he might as well be. "I looked it up. The lying, gaslighting, stonewalling, always twisting things around so it's *my* fault—it's emotional abuse."

"He hurt your *feelings*? Jesus, Sarah. Where'd you learn this from?"

"The internet."

"The internet," he repeats. "You don't go to counseling, but you go to the fucking internet for advice. Of course the internet's going to tell you what you want to hear."

"It's real. It's not in my head." But it feels like it's *physically* in her head, with the deafening thrum that booms *fight or flight*. "Just come get me. Please. Otherwise I'm stuck here for two weeks."

"Jesus. I'm looking up Sweetside, and it's over five hours away. Why don't you call Ben? He's closer. He's a good guy. I know he loves you."

Sarah's stomach turns, and she takes a deep breath, ready to play her last card. Graham might not believe her relationship troubles, but he'll understand the threat of strangers. "It's over with Ben. Can you *please* come get me? Everyone thinks I have the virus. They vandalized the motel I was staying at, and now I have to quarantine with a couple of local men." Her eyes prick with tears, although they're tears of frustration, not sadness. "I'm scared."

She means she's scared of being found, after what she did to Ben, but if Graham thinks she's talking about the Vass brothers, that works too. Graham lets out a resigned grunt. "Okay. If I leave after my morning class tomorrow, I can be in Sweetside in the afternoon. Where are you exactly?"

She gives him the directions. "Don't tell anyone I'm here. No one. Not even Ma-Ma and Ba-Ba. Please. I'll explain when I see you." She doesn't know how she's going to explain it, but she chokes out a final "Thanks" and slams down the receiver, her vision blurring with furious tears.

Elijah hands her a napkin. "Are you really scared of us? You don't have to be."

Sarah takes the napkin and dabs her eyes. "Not of you and Caleb. You've both been great." A voice at the back of her head whispers, *But what do they want? What do they want from you in exchange for kindness?* "I'm scared because of Ben, my boyfriend. *Ex*-boyfriend. The one I left in Toronto." In Toronto, howling with rage that she would dare leave him, as loud as winter wind through trees. The storm inside him, as Elijah had put it, unleashed with the savagery of a hurricane, threatening to drown her.

Until he'd seized her wrist hard enough to bruise, and she'd flailed in a panic, her fingers closing around the paring knife on the kitchen counter.

"He hurt you." Elijah's mouth is set, and at this moment, he doesn't look like either of his parents.

"It's not obvious. But he did. God, I wish he *had* hit me. Then maybe Graham would believe he was abusive." If her own brother doesn't believe her, how will the authorities believe she'd acted under stress?

"No you don't."

Sarah's lips part in chagrin. "Oh, Elijah. I'm so sorry. That was thoughtless of me." She puts a hand on his arm. His forearm is smaller than Caleb's, the muscles lean and wiry. His cheeks flush. She warms with compassion. Although Caleb might not have been touched by anyone other than family for months, it's possible Elijah's barely been touched at all, except in violence.

She withdraws her hand, but Elijah grabs it and squeezes gently. His paint-stained fingers are as cool as Caleb's are hot. His hands must be perpetually cold if he's always walking outside or in the unfinished sunroom. She almost regrets she'll be leaving tomorrow, because he could use a friend, and so could she.

"*I* believe you," he says. "There are ways you can hurt people without hitting them."

"Please don't tell Caleb. He might not understand."

"Of course I won't. So is your brother coming to get you?"

"Yes, thank God." She suspects Graham will try to convince her to go back to Toronto and stay with their parents, but that's a battle for another day. She'll borrow some money, rent a car, keep moving west to Calgary or Vancouver. Someplace with a high Asian population, where she can blend in.

Later, when Sarah returns to her room, she cuts herself as she stuffs the knife back in her bag. The washcloth shifted while in her pocket, and the exposed blade slices the pad of her thumb.

She finds a box of Band-Aids in the bathroom, wraps one around her thumb, and then settles on the recliner with *Macbeth*. She can't help feeling that ghostly presence standing over her shoulder again, but she forces herself not to look. She'll be leaving tomorrow, and Jacob Vass can have his room back.

When the windows begin to darken, a knock sounds on the door. "Room service," Caleb says. Sarah closes the book and laughs at his joking tone, because it's okay for him to be nice to her now. She'll be leaving Sweetside soon and will never see him again.

"Come in," she calls out.

Caleb tries the knob and opens the door. His eyes narrow above his mask. "You didn't lock it?"

"I guess I forgot," she says lightly.

His forehead scrunches as he lays the tray on the vanity. Sarah's mouth waters at the smell of marinara sauce and garlic bread. "Elijah didn't give you any trouble?" he asks.

"No, he's really nice."

The lines on Caleb's forehead deepen. *He has a storm inside him*, Elijah had said, and she can see it struggling to get out as keenly as she can feel the weight of Jacob Vass's legacy in the room.

He peers at Sarah's hands. "What happened to your thumb?"

"Paper cut. Nothing to worry about."

But when he leaves, saying, "Lock your door," he looks very worried indeed.

Sarah packs her bag that night to the soundtrack of the house. She imagines Sweetside Manor is telling her where its occupants are: Elijah's spry gait skipping down the stairs, probably heading to his studio, and Caleb's deliberate pace receding down the hall into his room.

She leaves the knife at the top of her backpack, just in case.

After she brushes her teeth, she switches off the light and climbs under the covers, floundering in the king-sized bed. She's not used to having so much space. A space in her bed means Ben's not home yet. Outside the darkened window, the wind whines, lonely and restless. She knows how it feels.

She only has to tiptoe down the hall and knock on Caleb's door. Just to see what would happen. After all, tomorrow, she'll never see him again.

But she doesn't, because she's learned from experience what happens when you get too close to charming men.

Her eyelids flutter closed, and the feeling she's not alone in the room settles on her breastbone like a sandbag. *Someone's been sleeping in my bed.* She tries to reach for the bedside lamp but can't lift her arms. There's someone in the room, a figure menacing in shadows as black and twisted as Elijah's painted trees. The ghost of Jacob Vass, of Ben, of men who would fit in the other half of the king-sized bed. As if she only exists in order for angry men to fill the space beside her.

Sarah opens her mouth to scream, but her tongue is a swollen slab of meat. The sound chokes in her throat, and she gags on the scent of stale tobacco. All she can hear is the howl of the wind and her strangled grunting as her voice batters her ribcage like a trapped bird.

The weight on her body lifts, and the scream finally tears from her lungs.

Sarah jolts upright, gasping for air. She's alone. *Alone, alone, alone,* the wind sings.

Footsteps skid down the hallway. A fist rattles the doorknob, thumps the door. "Sarah?" Caleb calls out.

"I'm okay." She scrambles out of bed, dashes to the door, and unlocks it. Caleb bursts in. He's not wearing a mask. His face is almost painful to look at, its planes cast in dramatic relief by the dim light.

His chest rises and falls as deeply as hers, straining against his shirt. "I'm okay," she repeats.

He touches her shoulder as if to reassure himself she's fine, his fingers warm and solid. Not like the apparition she thought she saw.

She wets dry lips. He's standing closer than the requisite six feet. "It was just a nightmare. I'm sorry I woke you up," she says.

His eyes dart behind her. "Don't be sorry. This room would give me nightmares, too. I'm glad you're safe." He squeezes her shoulder and drops his arm.

She smiles weakly. "I guess I was wrong. People can hear you scream out here after all."

Caleb tosses his head back and laughs, and Sarah's breath hitches. Say good night, she tells herself. She knows how this ends otherwise. "Thank you for coming to my rescue. Good night."

"Good night, Sarah," he says softly, and turns around and strides back down the hall.

She could follow him. But she doesn't. She closes the door, remembering to lock it. This time, when she falls asleep, she dreams of nothing.

CHAPTER SEVEN

He's not coming.

Sarah sits in the parlor on the florid orange and brown sofa, her jeans squeaking against the vinyl slipcover, one leg crossed over the other and jiggling impatiently. She's been waiting an hour and Graham isn't coming.

It would be just like him to let her stew in the mess she's made, to punish her for leaving Ben. A perverse way of getting back at his ex-wife. Something she said must have hit a nerve and dredged up the pain of losing Angie. All because she didn't *talk* to Ben. She bets Graham has never tried to reason with a compulsive liar.

Sarah's socks slide on the plastic floor runners as she switches legs. So many artifacts of death in the parlor. Desiccated plants and animals, living things plucked in their prime by long-dead hands. A bouquet of dried grass springs from a vase on the low coffee table. The antlers perch on a side table, the pointed prongs curved and polished like driftwood, reminding her of Elijah's pale fingers. Framed pressed flowers line the wood panel walls, and the stag's head sneers, judging her, telling her she doesn't belong.

Elijah prowls back and forth by the front window like a cat, occasionally peeking between the curtains. "I'm sorry to keep you from your painting," Sarah says, although she's not sorry. She's glad to have his company.

"There's always the chance to paint. Rarely the chance to meet someone new."

"You should go to art school. Then you can do both."

His face falls. "I wanted to go to OCAD after high school, but Caleb said he needed me to help run the motel."

She bites her lip in sympathy. "I'm sorry. You could take online classes?"

"Caleb would never install wifi up at the house. And anyway, he wouldn't like it. I don't do things Caleb doesn't like."

"You're talking to me now, aren't you?" she says, smiling.

"I *try* not to do things Caleb doesn't like." He looks down at his dirty fingernails. "But it's hard."

Sarah wants so much to give him a hug. First under the thumb of his father, and now Caleb. She identifies with him more than he knows. She'll regret leaving him here, this sad boy raised by men in a house of old, dead things. "You probably don't need art classes anyway. Have you shown your work anywhere besides the motel?"

"A gallery in Bracebridge wanted to put on a show a couple years ago, but Caleb wouldn't let me."

"That's ridiculous. You're what—in your mid-twenties? You're not a kid."

Elijah's mouth droops. "No, he's right. I'm better off at home."

"Do you want me to talk to him? I know I'm leaving, but I could call when I get to my brother's place. He might need an outsider's point of view."

"Well, you don't have to go right away. You could show your brother around. Does he like fishing or hiking? He might like to stay at the motel when it opens again."

She laughs. "Free advertising, huh? Caleb said he was planning to renovate the house and put it on Airbnb."

"Did he?" Elijah purses his lips. "That's strange. He's not good with visitors."

Sarah blinks, bewildered. "Really? He's been a very good host. Both of you have."

"You don't know him like I do. He's not as good with people as he seems."

Maybe Elijah's right. In the morning, Caleb was masked again and didn't mention her nightmare, only dropped off her breakfast and hastily excused himself to run errands. If he'd noticed her backpack zipped up and ready to go, he said nothing.

Sarah leans back, the sofa squeaking beneath her thighs. Elijah continues to pace. She wishes her phone worked so she could check the time. This ridiculous granny hunting lodge makes her feel like she's stuck in the past. Any minute, Grandma Sweet will totter into the room and tell her to sit up straight. Or worse, Jacob Vass will storm in with his hunting rifle and order her to get out. Who's to say it wasn't Jacob who crept out of the woods and painted that slur across her motel room? Anything to get the intruder to leave Sweetside. Or at least disappear from the Suicide Motel.

She can see why Caleb never took off the floor runners, the way Elijah skitters back and forth. He would've worn the varnish off the hardwood by now. Every movement Caleb makes is decisive, but Elijah is a coiled spring anxious to bounce. It's in his walk, and the frenetic power of his paintings. She can almost understand why his father hurt him. To control him, or maybe to try to harness that energy to his advantage.

Tires crunch on the driveway outside. Sarah jumps up. Elijah peeks out the window and freezes. "Oh no!"

Sarah's knees wobble. It's the police, finally. Or worse. "What is it?"

"Caleb's back. Go, before he sees you!"

Sarah whips up the stairs and into the main bedroom. She grabs the note and the cash she'd left that morning on the vanity and scrunches them into her pocket. Seizing a random book, she flops onto the recliner, her heartbeat scurrying at an unhappy pace. Why did Caleb have to come back early? *He's not good with visitors*, Elijah had said. She doesn't want to imagine what will happen when Graham shows up.

"Hi, Caleb!" Elijah calls out from downstairs, a little too loudly. He's letting her know Caleb's in the house. As if she doesn't recognize the whine of the front door and the strong, confident footfalls.

She doesn't hear Caleb's answer, remembering she forgot to lock the door, and he'll surely be up soon with her lunch. She scoots off the recliner and twists the lock, just as the stairs announce his movement.

The knock sounds on the door. Sarah counts to five, unlocks it, and flings it open. "Hi!" she says, a little too brightly. Her breath catches. He's not wearing a mask, and she'd never expected to see those cheekbones again.

His brow furrows. "You okay? You look a little flushed."

"Jumping jacks. I was feeling restless."

"Want to go out for a quick walk before lunch?"

"Sure."

Downstairs, she and Caleb pass Elijah as he slips into the kitchen. "Oh, hi Sarah," he says casually, as if they'd never spent the morning together. "I'm about to make sandwiches. Smoked turkey, okay?"

She nods. Caleb helps her into the parka, and then she laces up the borrowed boots and follows him out the door.

Outside, the air is clear and sharp as glass, cooling her heated cheeks. Her breath puffs into a white cloud, and she's suddenly very tired. Tired of having to wear a mask for people all the time. She hadn't realized how much she'd wanted Graham to show up, not just to take her away, but so she can be with someone with whom she doesn't have to pretend. As infuriating as he can be, she doesn't have to be *nice* to him. She can be herself, whoever that is. She's worn a mask for so long she doesn't know herself anymore.

"Is everything all right?" Caleb asks.

She forces a smile. She only has to be *nice* for a little while longer, until Graham comes. "I'm fine."

"How's your foot today?"

"It seems all right. I took the gauze off."

"Good. And your wrist?"

The skin is darkening like a winter sky, but she doesn't want to show him. "Can't do anything about bruises," she says, and stalks ahead to the backyard.

"Listen," Caleb says, catching up to her. "I know this is a scary time for you. Thrown in with a couple of strangers in a hostile town, right after you've left a bad relationship. You probably feel pretty powerless. I know I did, when—" He presses his lips together. "But if it helps, I want you to know you did the right thing, to leave. That took courage."

It's easy to be honest with him, now that she's going. "It didn't feel like courage." Only desperation. But maybe that's what courage is, doing the thing anyway, even though the blood pounds under your skin so hard you shake.

"It still was. I admire you for it. I wish I'd had it."

Sarah cranes her neck up at the woods. *If you disappeared, no one could hurt you anymore,* the trees seem to whisper as they sway in the wind. *You wouldn't have to figure out who to trust. You can trust us.*

Cottony clumps of snow float off the branches, so gently it's almost as if it's snowing again. She realizes she's never seen Caleb walk into the woods, only Elijah. Maybe Caleb knows if he goes in, he'll never come out. Like his father and the other victims of the Suicide Motel.

"You did the right thing, too," she says. She wonders if anyone ever told him that. Probably not. Maybe no one believed that Jacob Vass was hurting his sons, despite the evidence. There are so many ways for a pair of rambunctious boys to get hurt in the country. "You came back for Elijah."

"I hope you're right," he says, looking down at his hands.

"I actually wanted to talk to you about him."

He frowns. "Why?"

"He's such a gifted artist. I don't think he belongs here."

"Elijah's better off here. Trust me."

"Where he has bad memories? You must, too. You don't need to stay."

His jaw hardens. "This house belonged to Mom's family. I can't let Dad chase us away. It means he wins."

"You could at least let Elijah exhibit his work outside of Sweetside."

"I need him to help me with the motel."

"You could find someone else."

Caleb's nostrils flare. "I told you, they treat us like outsiders here. We're the town weirdos, and no one wants to work at the Suicide Motel. Our last housekeeper only stayed as long as she did because she was friends with Mom."

"Hire someone from outside of town."

"Why would anyone outside of town want to live in Sweetside?" He spins to face her. "Would *you* want to stay here?"

She knows it's a hypothetical question, but it knocks the breath out of her lungs. She freezes, her eyes locked with his.

The sound of a car pulling up out front interrupts her answer.

Graham. Finally. He must've gotten lost, or delayed by his students. Sarah turns away from Caleb and rushes around the house, shoulders slumping with relief because she would've said yes. If Caleb asked her to stay again with those blue, blue eyes, she would say yes.

She falls back when she sees the black and white of a police cruiser.

Caleb comes up behind her, so close his breath skims her ear as he swears. "Shit." Then he strides forward. "Uncle Isaac!"

The driver-side door opens. The policeman who'd confronted her when her car had broken down unfolds himself from the seat. He's wearing a mask, but she reads suspicion in his face anyway. Now that she's seen the photo of Jacob Vass, she can tell Isaac is his brother. His eyes are deep-set, like Caleb's, and they share Jacob's long, hard squint.

"Caleb. What's *she* doing outside? And why are neither of you wearing masks?"

"She needed to stretch her legs. Don't worry, we're taking precautions. Do you want some lunch? Elijah's making sandwiches. Or can we get you a coffee?"

Isaac shakes his head. "I'm good. This isn't a social call."

Dread pools in the pit of Sarah's belly. Isaac sticks his thumbs in his belt loops, calling attention to the gun holster at his hip. "There's been an incident in town. An Oriental man—"

"Uncle Isaac, you can't say 'Oriental.' It's *Asian*."

Isaac gives Caleb a hard look. "An *Asian* man stopped at the Timmy's drive-thru and got himself mobbed. Jerry smashed his back windshield, and Old Man Doherty shot out a tail light."

Sarah's hand flies to her mouth. Isaac's gaze flits towards her, and she drops her arm, lacing her fingers together in a demure posture.

"Needless to say, the *Asian* high-tailed it out of there, going north. Dumbfuck should've known better than to drop into a strange town. Anyway, I dropped by to see if the young lady here knows anything about this visitor."

"Uncle Isaac, just because Sarah's Asian too doesn't mean—"

"She did say she was heading north to visit family."

Sarah pastes on a pleasant but puzzled smile. "My phone's dead. I haven't been able to call anyone."

"It's true. I don't have the right charging cable. She's been under radio silence," Caleb says.

"You swear?"

"I swear, Uncle Isaac."

Isaac nods. "All right. I believe you, Caleb. But if I catch her outside again, we will have to take measures."

"Uncle Isaac—"

Isaac jabs a finger at him. "*Measures*. And I will consider you and Elijah compromised, too. I can't show favoritism, even if it'll break your Aunt Judy's heart."

Caleb bows his head. "Yes, sir."

"Good boy." Isaac tips his hat. "Take her inside now. Tell Elijah I said hi."

"Go," Caleb murmurs.

Sarah scurries up the porch steps and into the house. The door swings shut behind her, but she can still feel Isaac's glare on her back, measuring the target she can never take off.

CHAPTER EIGHT

Sarah scrapes her feet on the doormat, boots feeling like they're made of lead. "Was that Uncle Isaac?" Elijah calls from the kitchen.

"He says hi," she says weakly.

"Guess he wasn't happy to see you outside."

Sarah mumbles an assent as she slips off the coat. She hopes Graham is okay. He can't be hurt if he'd driven off. She feels a rare surge of affection toward him. He came to pick her up after all. But he can't again. He might call the police, but like Isaac, they'll probably tell him it was his fault for stopping in a strange town during a pandemic.

The door swings open again, admitting Caleb and a frigid blast that slaps Sarah's already numb cheeks. Caleb turns the deadbolt into place, his ear to the door. When the sound of Isaac's car fades, he turns on Sarah, blazing with a fire she's never seen before. "Did you call your brother?"

Sarah backs up through the dining room to the kitchen. Jacob Vass's laughing face taunts her from the wall of photographs. "No, I—"

"What's going on?" Elijah says.

"Nothing, Elijah. Did you call your brother? After I asked you not to?"

"I—" She can't find the words. She doesn't want to lie, can't lie when his glare has her pinned like a butterfly under glass. Elijah had said Caleb had a storm inside him, but it's not a raincloud, it's a cloudless sky that's too bright to look at. Fierce and hot and impossible to hide from.

"Shit." He yanks off his jacket and slams it over a dining chair.

"I'll pay for the long distance—"

"It's not that. You nearly got your brother killed. What were you thinking? Especially after what those assholes did at the motel? What do you think they would've done to *you* if I hadn't shown up?"

It seems stupid now, especially when Caleb's reasons are perfectly valid. After everything that happened to her, she hadn't stopped to think it might happen to Graham, too.

"It's not her fault. I told her she could call him," Elijah blurts out.

Caleb looks at Elijah, and for a single, terrifying second, Sarah can see Jacob Vass in his face. Something incandescent flares in his eyes, and he shoulders past her into the kitchen.

In one brutal motion, he tears the phone off the wall and slams it on the table.

Both Sarah and Elijah jump at the noise. Half the plug sticks out of the socket, snapped off by Caleb's wrath. "Fuck," Caleb says, gripping the back of a chair, and Sarah's terrified he's going to break that too. "*Fuck.*"

Sarah inches backward until she's standing in the doorway. This is the man who can't be trusted with knives. She sees it now. *Go,* the voice at the back of her head urges over the roar in her ears. *Just go.* It's the same voice that whispered to her when Ben had slumped over the kitchen counter, blood seeping between his fingers as he clamped his hand to his neck.

The fury drains from Caleb's face, and he's Caleb again, not his father. "Oh God. I'm sorry, Sarah. It's not because of you. I should've done this years ago."

He glances at Elijah.

"He didn't do anything!" Sarah rushes forward to stand in front of Elijah, who quivers like a rabbit.

Caleb's shoulders go limp. "No. Of course not. Sarah, please return to your room. You shouldn't be down here. It's for your own safety."

"Will you be okay?" she asks Elijah.

"He's fine," Caleb says.

"I was asking Elijah, not you," she snaps.

Both brothers look surprised at her outburst. Caleb straightens and lifts his chin. The fire in his eyes has extinguished, and he regards her with a cool, assessing gaze. She's done it now. She's shown herself. Revealed a bit of the stress that's been boiling inside her for so long. She's no longer *nice.*

"I'm fine, Sarah," Elijah says. "Go. He's right. You shouldn't be down here."

Sarah looks from Elijah to Caleb. A vein throbs at Caleb's temple, but his fists have uncurled from the chair. Elijah crosses his arms and nods.

Go. Just go. She plods out of the kitchen and drags her feet up the stairs.

Caleb's voice rises from the kitchen when she reaches the landing. "Why did you let her make that call?"

Holding her breath, Sarah closes her door—from the outside—and shuffles back to the top of the stairs, praying the house won't give her away.

"So her brother could come. What's the harm?"

"You know we can't have people here. What if—" Caleb's voice chokes off. "We can't let Dad win. I'm only trying to protect you."

"I can protect myself," Elijah says stubbornly.

"I know you can. But—"

The railing squeaks under Sarah's trembling hands.

"Shush," says Caleb. "What was that?"

A chair scrapes against the kitchen floor. Sarah flies down the hall and slips back into her room. She locks the door, wincing at the tell-tale click.

She recognizes this part. The honeymoon phase is over. Everything is great until it's not, and you wonder what you did wrong and how you can get the good feelings back.

You know what you did wrong, a voice says in the back of her head.

It sounds like Ben.

She collapses into the recliner. Her nose wrinkles at the musty scent, but she doesn't want to get up again. She wants to sink into the upholstery as if it's quicksand and never come out. Let the spirits of Jacob Vass and Stuart McGee and Joseph Singh lure her into the woods. Then no one will be able to find her, least of all Ben's ghost. She'll finally be free.

The wind whistles outside the windows. It sounds less like screaming now, and more like singing. Sarah glances down at *Bulfinch's Mythology*, splayed open at the page about the Sirens. Odysseus had asked his men to tie him to the ship's mast so their song wouldn't tempt him to his doom. Maybe that's why Caleb and Elijah keep telling her to lock the door and stay inside the house. Otherwise the woods will claim her too.

A rap sounds on the door. "Sarah?" Caleb says. "I've got your lunch."

She doesn't want to talk to him. She wants to be left alone and let the wind and the woods devour her troubles. "Just leave it outside."

His leaden sigh penetrates the wall between them. "I'm sorry. I overreacted. Could you please open the door? I'd like to apologize to your face."

He sounds tired, and that's what convinces Sarah to slide off the recliner. Ben never sounded tired. His rage drew from a bottomless well. And he certainly never apologized unless he had no options left.

Sarah unlocks the door and lets Caleb in. He crosses the room and sets a tray on the vanity. He hasn't put a mask on. There doesn't seem to be any point now. Somewhere, they've crossed a line, and the air she breathes is the same he and Elijah breathe.

"I'm sorry. I shouldn't have yelled at you," he says.

She doesn't respond, only waits for him to make excuses, to blame her. It's always her fault, isn't it?

But it *was* her fault. She phoned Graham when he'd asked her not to.

He's not like Ben, she reminds herself.

But what if he is?

But what if he isn't?

Sarah stands rooted to the spot, hands suddenly sweaty, paralyzed by the electricity of attraction and fear.

"And I know what I did with the phone was excessive. But I'm scared for Elijah. You don't know him like I do. He's not as good with people as he seems."

He drags a hand down his face. Lines bracket his downturned mouth, and he resembles his mother more than his father now. "And I'm scared for you, too. Your brother could've been killed. That's not an exaggeration. Old Man Doherty really thinks the virus is a Chinese conspiracy to undermine his way of life. As if China cares about his shitty pool hall." He snorts.

She can't help but smile at that. He smiles back.

Make nice. Accept the apology, because otherwise, the storm will break again. And it actually was her fault.

"No, I'm the one who's sorry. I shouldn't have called Graham." She's careful to keep her face contrite. "I'm becoming too much of a nuisance. I should just go."

"Are you in a hurry to leave?" He smiles again, and her stomach flutters with yearning and dread.

"No, of course not. But there's no chance of my car getting fixed soon?"

He shakes his head. "Lars is in bad shape, and half of his staff tested positive. Uncle Isaac's furious."

"Is there a bus I could take to Timmins?"

"The bus stop's in the middle of town, across from the Tim Horton's."

Where Graham got shot at. The color drains from her face. Caleb adds, "Sarah, if there's anything you want or need to make your stay here more comfortable, you only have to ask. Let me know what I can do. I want you to be happy."

There's only one thing that will make her happy. "Help me get out of Sweetside."

"You know I can't do that," he says, sadly. He turns and ambles for the doorway, his keys jangling from the carabiner on his belt loop. Like a jailer.

"Lock your door," is the last thing he says, but she doesn't see the point. She's trapped here anyway.

CHAPTER NINE

It snows again the next morning, because of course it does. Sarah lingers in bed long after the windows brighten, staring at the flurry of white. She can't see the woods from where she lies, but the trees creak as gloomily as Sweetside Manor's floorboards.

She needs to leave.

She needs to leave before they find Ben's body, before they find her. Before she reveals any more of herself to Caleb. She came too close yesterday, when she'd practically begged him to help her get out of Sweetside. It was the wrong move. Now he knows how desperate she is. It's always safer when they think she's a nice girl who won't cause trouble.

The flurries fade into drifting flakes, and she thinks about getting up. Maybe she can hitch a ride north. Maybe she can walk there in Elijah's borrowed boots. Sling on her backpack and disappear.

And then she wonders if the other small towns she might pass through will be just as welcoming to anyone who looks like her.

Caleb and Elijah are her best chance for survival. For now.

Sarah's heart skips a beat as the house sings Caleb's theme song: the strong tread up the stairs, followed by a confident knock. She struggles to sit up. "Come in," she says.

The door opens, admitting the soothing scent of coffee and aftershave. Caleb says, "You should've—"

"Locked the door. Yes. Whatever." She picks at an imaginary wrinkle in the quilt.

"It's for your own safety. You know what the people of Sweetside are capable of."

His overprotectiveness seems so pointless. A locked door won't keep out a rifle shot. "You don't need to helicopter over me like you do with Elijah."

"You don't know anything about Elijah. Or me, for that matter."

Her chin snaps up at the sudden sharpness of his words. She doesn't want to look at him, but can't help it. She savors his straight nose, the inviting divot in his upper lip, the square jawbone that dominates his face. The shadows under his eyes bring out the vivid blue of his irises. She's glad he didn't sleep well either.

"No," she says quietly. "No, I guess I don't."

Caleb deposits the breakfast tray on the vanity. "I'm going out to clear the snow. Do *not* leave the room." His face softens, the dark brows drawing together. "I don't want you to get hurt. You've been through so much already."

When she answers tersely with a nod, he lumbers away and closes the door behind him. She frowns. Something about him is off this morning. The way he'd come in and left didn't sound right.

He wasn't wearing his keys.

Sarah launches herself out of bed and quietly opens the door. She creeps down the hall to the top of the stairs and catches a glimpse of Caleb's broad back disappearing through the front door.

She bolts to his room, her pulse counting the seconds before he returns to the house. The door is ajar, and this time, she has no scruples about entering. The bed is neatly made, the copy of *Of Mice and Men* sitting on the bedside table. A flannel shirt and a pair of jeans hang over a chair. She checks the belt loops and pockets but finds nothing. The top of the dresser is bare except for a handful of change. Where else would he drop his keys after coming home for the night?

She yanks the bedside table drawer open but finds only batteries and random cables. "Damn it," she mutters.

"Are you looking for his keys?"

She jumps, her pulse fluttering like paper. Elijah leans against the doorframe. "Are you looking for the keys to the truck?" he asks again. "He doesn't keep them in his room."

Sarah laughs nervously and shuts the drawer. "No, you caught me being nosy. He doesn't talk much about himself."

"He hides them from me, too."

She can't lie to that sad, guileless face. Maybe Elijah can help. "I need to get out of Sweetside. Where does he keep them? He didn't have them on his belt this morning."

"I don't know. I've looked everywhere."

"Downstairs? How long does it take to shovel the driveway?"

"The snowblower's quick, but he'll probably clear the motel parking lot too."

"Great." Sarah hurries down the stairs and circles the ground floor. She runs her fingers across the spines of the books in the dining room china hutch. Jams her hands between the sofa cushions in the den. Checks every corner of the kitchen's stained laminate counters. She even searches the parlor in case the carabiner is hiding under a crocheted doily.

"I don't think you'll find them," Elijah says, trailing at her heels. "I never have."

"Why would he want to hide them from you?"

"He doesn't want me to leave. It's for my own good."

Her mouth flattens. "That's what they always say."

"No, he's right. I'm not like other people."

Ben had told her she wasn't like anyone else either, when they'd first started dating.

"I don't like to upset him," he says, his mouth drooping. He's like a bird who's never flown outside his cage. This life is all he knows. It's safe—to some extent. Predictable. Sarah knows how he feels. "You know what it's like, right? What you said about your ex. You *know*. Walking on eggshells all the time, making a show of being harmless, so you don't make him mad. Does it work? For you?"

"I—" Does it? She was nice to Isaac and Jerry, and someone still spray-painted the C-word on her motel room door. "I don't know."

He tips his head to the side. "That's the garage closing. Caleb's done. Go. Don't forget to lock your door."

Sarah dashes back up the stairs. She shuts the door, locks it. Leaning against the wall, she shuts her eyes, gulping for air. She's no good to anyone, especially herself, if she succumbs to panic. Panic is what got her into this mess in the first place.

"Elijah!" Caleb calls out. "I'm going into town. Can you take care of Sarah's lunch?"

"Sure thing, I'll see you later," Elijah yells back, and Sarah knows it's for her benefit.

She doesn't slink back downstairs, though. There's no point, since Caleb has taken the truck. She takes her time getting dressed, leaving the pajamas crumpled on the unmade bed, and starts in on breakfast. The blueberry muffin Caleb left feels chalky in her mouth. She washes it down with cold coffee without tasting it, thoughts churning.

She'll find a way to leave. She got out of a bad situation once, she can do it again. She rescues her wrinkled pajamas, folds them up, and stuffs them into the backpack. Ben's death showed her she can be resourceful and act quickly. She only needs to be ready when the opportunity strikes.

The doorbell rings.

She hadn't heard a car pulling up; she'd been in the bathroom brushing her teeth. The doorbell rings again. Multiple chimes announce the caller's impatience. She holds her breath, feeling like a kid pretending no one's home while her parents are out.

Sarah creeps to the front windows but doesn't recognize the sedan parked in the driveway. The porch roof hides whoever's at the door. Graham could've finally traded in his old SUV. Or maybe Isaac sent someone to check up on her. Or maybe it's Old Man Doherty and Jerry the tow truck driver and everyone else they could rustle up, bearing torches and pitchforks to drive the interloper out of town.

The doorbell rings a third time, the caller pressing it for a full ten seconds. They won't take no for an answer. The house comes alive as Elijah begins to move through it. Sarah tiptoes to the bedroom door and listens, breath thickening with dread.

A few minutes later, Elijah calls out, "Sarah! You have a visitor!"

Sarah sags against the door, relieved. It's Graham. Who else would be so annoyingly insistent? He's managed to come back for her without attracting notice from the townspeople. She unlocks the door and hurries down the hallway.

When she's halfway down the stairs, Elijah steps away from the man standing in the foyer.

The man raises his masked face. Sarah clings to the railing, her knees buckling beneath her.

He's alive.

"Hello, Sarah," Ben says.

CHAPTER TEN

Sarah finds her voice, although it sounds distant above the panicked thundering of her pulse. She'd been sure he was dead. And how did he even find her? "What are you doing here?"

"Is that any way to talk to your fiancé? We were supposed to get married in the summer," he tells Elijah, "but then the pandemic hit."

Sarah's gut clenches. If she doesn't get down these stairs immediately, her sweaty hands will slip off the railing and she'll tumble to his feet. They've discussed marriage, but he can't hold down a job long enough to afford a ring, let alone a wedding. "What are you doing here?" she repeats.

Ben rolls his eyes at Elijah as if to say, *Women, amirite?* "Graham called me. Said you were stuck in this podunk town and needed to be rescued."

Sarah feels like she's going to throw up. Caleb was right. She should've never called Graham.

"Can I take your coat?" Elijah says.

She wants to say, *No, he's not staying* but it's too late. Ben sheds his coat and hands it to Elijah, his eyes never leaving her. He hands over his scarf as well, revealing a rust-stained patch of gauze on his neck, in the spot where her knife had sliced.

"I've already introduced myself to your host," Ben says. "Is there somewhere Sarah and I can talk, Elijah?"

She doesn't like the way he says Elijah's name, like he's already best buddies with him. Elijah's hers.

"You can use the parlor. Would you like a coffee?" Elijah asks.

"Sure. Milk and sugar."

"Sarah?"

"No, thank you."

She watches helplessly as Elijah's back retreats into the dining room. Ben grasps her upper arm and steers her into the parlor. "Holy shit. I'm at Oma's house," he says.

He sits on the sofa and pats the seat beside him, looking up expectantly as if she's a dog. She doesn't even want to be in the same house as him, but her body moves on autopilot. It's best to do what he wants. The easiest way to deal with him. She sets her face into neutral. *Look at me. I'm boring. I'm not worth it.*

Does it work? For you? Elijah had asked. Sarah prays it will.

Ben takes off his mask. Sarah once thought him good-looking, but now the sight of his face makes her sick. She guesses the gash she'd opened under his jawline has been stitched up. If the police aren't here to charge her with assault or attempted manslaughter, what excuse did he make at the hospital? Though it doesn't matter. He'll make up a new story once it scars, a story he can use to impress someone or gain their sympathy. A hockey fight, or a mark left by his old man, depending on who he talks to.

"You missed any major arteries, thank God. The hospital said it looked more serious than it was." He leans toward Sarah, resting his elbows on his knees. "I suppose I only have myself to blame. I scared you when I grabbed your wrist."

It's one of the few true things he's ever said.

His voice lowers. "But I was afraid of losing you."

His eyes bore into hers. He's probably been watching romance movies again to get the look right. The way he shifts the blame to her only makes her nauseous. It's *her* fault he feels the way he does. It's always her fault.

Elijah chooses that moment to enter. He sets Ben's coffee on the side table next to the decorative antlers. Ben straightens, his jaw twitching. Sarah silently thanks Elijah for interrupting.

Elijah gawks at the gauze on Ben's neck. "Shaving accident," Ben says. His smile is easy, like a worn-in baseball cap that comes on or off, depending on the company. Sarah was once charmed by that smile, until she saw how quickly it disappeared after Ben got what he wanted.

When Elijah doesn't leave, Ben's jaw twitches again but he continues. "I know these are trying times. The two of us, cooped up in that little place—I get why you freaked out. I forgive you. Come home, Sarah. We've been together too long to throw away what we have."

His voice is even and reasonable. Sarah's own words choke in her mouth. She wants to tell him *It's over.* Just two little words, but they're stuck in her throat like fishbones. *Get out.* Another two little words, but she's terrified of how he might react. She ran from his wrath once; she has nowhere left to run, except the woods.

Her palms stick to the sofa's vinyl slipcover. Her terror is a bubble expanding behind her sternum, hindering her breath and speech. It's the same fear that took control of her body when he'd caught her in the apartment kitchen with her go-bag.

"I don't think she wants to leave," Elijah says.

Ben turns on Elijah, his smile deepening. "What did she tell you?"

Elijah comes forward, his long fingers clutching the back of the armchair. "That you abused her."

"Did she tell you I hit her?" Ben splutters, more astonished than outraged. He rounds on Sarah. "Did you tell him I *hit* you?"

She shakes her head, still unable to form words. Elijah says, "The lying. Cheating. Gaslighting."

"When did I do that?" Ben asks her, disbelief clouding his face.

"All the time," she croaks. "He's doing it now."

Ben laughs and shakes his head. "Come on. Give me some examples."

"That—that time you bought those expensive headphones and hid them from me." The incident falls limply from her stiff tongue. It seems such a small thing. But it's been a barrage of these seemingly insignificant transgressions, gathering like raindrops in a bucket, and she never noticed until the water level went over her head and she started to drown.

"Well, of course. You would've gotten mad." He looks at Elijah again, his eyebrows raised like, *Can you believe what you're hearing?* Elijah's face is wide-eyed but impassive. Sarah's glad Ben is talking to Elijah and not Caleb, because it would break her heart if Caleb were standing there, nodding.

She clears her throat. "And when you told me you'd quit smoking, and I came home and the toilet was filled with cigarette butts."

"I told you, I have no idea how those got there."

"And before the pandemic, there were all the times I came home, and it smelled like baby powder."

"Oh my God, it was probably the neighbor's perfume."

"And the curtains were closed."

"I don't remember that. Are you sure you're not mixing it up with some other nights?" He glances at Elijah. "I don't know what she told you, but you can see it's all in her head."

"I know what I saw," she says, teeth gritting.

"Well, you saw wrong. Anyway, I have some good news. I got a new job. I'm starting in a couple of weeks. I figure we can take that time to work on our relationship."

So gracious, so reasonable. So terrifying.

"If the job works out, I can save some money and we can finally buy a place." She's heard that line before. "We both work from home now, so we don't have to stay in Toronto. We could go where it's cheaper. We could even buy a house like this. This is a great property, by the way," he adds, turning to Elijah.

"You should see the woods out back," Elijah says.

Ben wants to move her away from the safety of the city, to where it's cheaper and lonelier and what few friends Sarah has left will abandon her for good. "I'm not going with you," she says, trying to keep her voice from shaking.

Ben sighs and passes his hand over his face. When he looks up again, his eyes are red.

"I miss you, Sarah. I'm miserable without you. Come home."

Sarah's belly sours. He's offering love, or what he thinks is the love she wants. He thinks she wants to be needed. To feel as special as he first claimed she was. Earlier this year, he would've been right. But after those long months trapped together, she sees he actually needs *her*, to fuck and to pay the rent and soothe his feelings and entertain him when he's bored. Because without her attention, he's just another angry man blustering into the void.

She bets he *is* miserable, and not for the reason he wants her to believe.

She shakes her head, slowly. "No." She has to remain calm, as inscrutable as the stag on the wall. Let him think she's small and boring. She can't give him the drama he craves.

Color starts to stain Ben's cheeks. He rises to his feet and stabs a finger at Elijah. "Is it because of him? Are you fucking him? Seriously, you accuse me of cheating, and you turn around and fuck this loser?"

He wants her to react so he can justify his temper. She blinks calmly. "No."

"I think it's time for you to go, Ben." Elijah's voice quavers, and Sarah feels an enormous rush of tenderness toward him. He's standing up for her even though he's had his share of angry men.

Ben gestures to the gauze on his neck. "I could've gone to the police. I could've told the doctors you attacked me. But I didn't. I made up a bullshit story about the knife slipping when I was slicing a bagel. I did it for you."

Sarah bites her tongue to keep herself from responding. No, he did it for himself. Because he'd never tell anyone his girlfriend had walked out on him so dramatically. They'd want to know why.

"It's time," Elijah repeats, coming around the armchair.

Ben whirls toward him. "Are you going to stop me from taking her home?"

"Maybe."

Elijah's face brightens for a split second before Ben drives his fist into it.

Elijah crumples into the armchair. Sarah forgets her composure and jumps up from the sofa. She digs her fingers into Ben's arm, trying to drag him away. "Ben, stop it!" she shouts.

Ben shakes her off and straightens his collar. "See? See what you made me do?" Because it's always her fault, isn't it?

Elijah begins to laugh, his shoulders shaking while he drools blood down the front of his shirt.

"What the fuck are you laughing about?" Ben says.

"Go on," Elijah says, struggling to stand. "Is that all you've got?"

"Ben, don't!" Sarah cries, but he ignores her. He grabs Elijah by the front of his shirt, half-lifting him off the armchair, and punches him again.

When Elijah staggers to his feet, eyes shining, he asks, "Do you hear the screaming?" and she's not sure if he's asking her or Ben. "Do you?"

"You little freak," Ben snarls, clamping his hands around Elijah's neck.

"Don't touch him!" Sarah grabs at Ben again, but he shoulders her backward, sending her tumbling over the coffee table. She grunts as she hits the floor, stars exploding behind her eyes. The vase tips off the edge and rolls across the plastic runners, spilling dried grass everywhere.

Elijah makes a horrible choking sound as he claws helplessly at Ben's shoulders. He's ripped off the gauze but can't do anything else. The bubble of terror behind Sarah's ribs pops. Ben can't hurt Elijah, not when he's been hurt so much already. She struggles to her feet, snatches up the vase in both hands, and smashes it over Ben's head.

Ben lets go of Elijah and puts a hand to his temple, gaping with disbelief as it comes away red.

The disbelief quickly twists into fury. "This has gone on far enough," he thunders. He seizes Sarah's wrist, the one he already left his mark on. She hisses from the pain as he yanks her toward him. The roar battering her eardrums is so loud she's afraid they'll burst. "It doesn't have to be like this. Why are you treating me this way? What have I done to deserve—"

Elijah splashes Ben's coffee into his face. Ben releases Sarah, and she crashes back to the floor.

Ben swears, wiping his eyes with his sleeve. "You little shit," he growls, shoving Elijah over the coffee table.

Elijah drops the mug and tumbles onto the broken pottery. Ben starts to kick him. "You think you can—" *Kick.* "Take her—" *Kick.*

Elijah curls into a ball and keens in a high-pitched voice, suddenly transformed into the little boy whose dad was always a bit rough. A dark and molten fever floods across Sarah's skin.

"Away—" *Kick.* "From—"

The thudding in Sarah's eardrums is unbearable. She gropes for the side table and as she pulls herself up, her hand skims over the decorative antlers, just the right size for her fingers to curve around.

"Me." *Kick.*

The pressure in her ears detonates, and she swings the antlers as hard as she can. She swings and when she pulls back, the antlers catch on something, and when she tugs, blood sprays all over her as she almost falls backward again. Ben clutches the side of his neck like he did that morning she fled the apartment, his eyes bulging in surprise.

This time she didn't miss an artery.

And because the sight of Ben's face makes her sick, even if it's smeared with blood and shock, she regains her balance and swings a second time, and a third, screaming herself raw because no one can hear you scream out here.

She screams until she becomes conscious of a body behind hers, slim but strong. Long, cool fingers cover hers, and she registers the slickness of the antlers in her hands. "Sarah," Elijah says gently. "You can stop now."

Ben gurgles in a glossy puddle on the sofa. She pants furiously, tasting his blood on her lips, and it just enrages her that even as he's dying, he's pushing part of himself, unwanted, on her body.

Elijah pries the antlers out of her grip and sets them on the sofa beside Ben.

"Were you really getting married?" His left eye is starting to swell, but it's still bright and curious.

"No, that was another one of his lies. Oh God. I didn't mean to—"

Yes, she did.

"I would've done the same," he says.

"Are you okay?" She reaches out and touches Elijah's cheek, leaving a streak of red.

He grins, revealing bloodied teeth. "I've had worse. Are *you* okay? How do you feel?"

"I'm fine." How does she feel?

She feels free.

She feels alive.

She feels safe, at last.

Her heart pounds but it's a fierce, triumphant drumbeat.

The feeling doesn't last, though. The implication of what she's done crashes over her head like a tidal wave. "Oh my God. We need to call 911."

Elijah puts his hand over her sticky one. "No one has to know," he says, quietly.

Because she trusts him, she swallows and nods. "Yes. No one has to know."

And then they hear the rumble of Caleb's truck outside.

Sarah and Elijah stare at each other. There's no way they can hide Ben's body and clean up the parlor in time.

The front door opens. "Hey Elijah, whose car is—"

Time stops. Every heartbeat is a thunderclap, each breath an explosion. Sarah feels every splash of blood sliding down her hair, soaking into her clothes, congealing on her skin. Elijah's breath shudders, wet and labored.

"Elijah," Caleb says, slowly. "Elijah, what did you do?"

CHAPTER ELEVEN

"Sarah, are you all right?" Caleb asks.

"It's not her blood," Elijah says. He steps to the side, revealing their uninvited guest. Ben stares up at the stag's head, his mouth gaping as if he's about to comment on it. There's blood everywhere. Pooled on the sofa and the floor, splattered across the walls and tables. Sarah smells it cooking on the radiator. There's even a little splash on the stag's mouth, making it look feral.

Only dead things in this room, Sarah thinks, a tremor starting to ripple in her gut.

"Who's that?" Caleb demands.

"It's Ben," Sarah says.

"Who the fuck is Ben?"

"My ex."

"Elijah," Caleb says.

"He didn't do it!" she says. "It was me. He was beating up Elijah. I couldn't let him—" Her shoulders shake. The relief of Ben being dead ebbs away, and she realizes it's not relief, only adrenaline, and she vomits over the scatter of broken pottery and dried grass.

"I'm sorry," she says, wiping her mouth and realizing too late she's only smearing blood across her face. She's sorry Caleb has seen her like this.

"Wait here," Caleb says.

Where does he think she's going to go? He turns on his heel and returns outside. Probably to call his uncle. She hugs herself, the stench of iron and bile and coffee searing her nostrils. She'd throw up from the smell if not for her now-empty stomach. Does Caleb believe it was self-defense? He must know *she* couldn't have given Elijah a black eye.

Elijah reaches out and rests a hand on her shoulder. The weight keeps her from shattering again.

The front door opens. The chill from outside licks at Sarah's damp, clammy skin. Caleb enters the foyer and drops a roll of plastic sheeting and a bucket on the floor. He shucks off his jacket, slings it on the staircase railing, and rolls up his sleeves like he's done this a million times before.

"Is anyone going to miss this asshole?" Caleb gestures toward Ben.

Sarah shakes her head numbly. "He doesn't start a new job for a couple of weeks."

"Friends? Family?"

"He doesn't have any close friends, and he doesn't talk much to his family. He doesn't have a good relationship with them." He didn't have good relationships with anyone. Why did she expect it would be different with her? So many red flags she should've seen before it was too late, before it ended in bruises and blood.

Caleb nods. "Good. He'll be another victim of the Suicide Motel."

"You're not going to call the police?" she asks, and is immediately ashamed of the hope in her voice.

"Do you want me to?" Caleb's eyes are hard and serious, like glass. "I'd rather not have the cops all over here, for Elijah's sake. But if you want me to call Uncle Isaac, I will."

"They'll think I did it, won't they?" Elijah shifts from foot to foot. "Because they think I'm weird. I touched the antlers too."

Caleb raises his eyebrows. "Is that what you used?" He puts his hands on his hips and looks from Elijah to Sarah to Ben—no, to the *body*. He heaves a sigh. "I don't know what they'll think."

"Don't call them." Sarah doesn't have to think twice. She can't let Elijah suffer for her actions. And Ben deserves to be forgotten. To disappear.

"Okay. Here's what we're going to do." Caleb pulls a garbage bag from the bucket. "Sarah," he says, tossing it to her. "Go upstairs and have a shower. Put your dirty clothes in there. We can try to wash them or—"

"Toss them." She doesn't want to see that hoodie ever again.

A fistful of latex gloves and an industrial-sized bottle of bleach follow the garbage bag. "Elijah and I will take care of the body. We'll put it in the garage. Unfortunately, the ground's frozen, so we'll have to wait until spring to bury it."

It, as if Ben is a thing and no longer a person. Because he *is* just a thing now. Whoever Ben was, he's not the length of meat and bone stretched out on their grandmother's couch.

Caleb tugs on a pair of latex gloves and hands another pair to Elijah. Elijah's face looks worse than Ben's, but at least he's alive. Caleb starts to unroll the plastic drop cloth outside of the parlor. "We'll put him in the chest freezer and cover him in road salt. If the power goes out, the salt will help if he starts to decompose, but he should stay frozen in the garage all winter."

The idea of Ben frozen in this moment, forever preserved as the vicious man who tried to hurt her and Elijah, terrifies Sarah more than he did when he was alive.

"Sarah," Caleb says, noticing she hasn't moved. The steel in his eyes bends a little. "It's going to be okay. Now go. Elijah and I will take care of this."

"Go," Elijah says, pulling on the latex gloves.

Sarah runs upstairs, careful not to touch the railing with her sticky hands, and the steps groan under her feet like a dying man.

Ben is dead.

Sarah wrenches the shower's hot water faucet until the bathroom clouds with steam. She opens her mouth and rinses away the bile and sick, scrubbing behind her gums with the fingers of her left hand. The fingers that didn't touch the antlers. If she scrubs hard enough, maybe she can also wash away the taste of Ben's blood. But it's too late. The memory is branded inside her, as unwanted as a parasite. She imagines it burrowing deep inside her belly and curling up like a fetus. The storm inside him, now brewing inside her.

Ben is dead, and she's alone.

And because no one can watch her in the bathroom, not even Jacob Vass's ghost, she braces herself against the ugly shower tiles and laughs and laughs as Ben's blood swirls down the drain.

After the water runs clear, Sarah gets dressed and pads downstairs, cradling a garbage bag heavy with her blood-soaked clothes. A chill settles into her bones as air currents sweep through her wet hair. Caleb must have opened a window or door. The house is breathing. After months, possibly years of being sealed in a bubble—like the sunroom—Sweetside Manor has opened up and come to life.

And she was the first cut, letting the infection in. *Someone's been sleeping in my bed.*

The house creaks, drawing icy air from the outside. It inhales. Exhales. Inhales again. The draft carries the sting of bleach on its back. It scorches the inside of Sarah's nostrils and the back of her throat. She approaches the parlor, shielding her nose and mouth with her hand as the smell intensifies. The house murmurs as snow strafes the front windows.

Ben's body and the plastic drop cloth are gone. A rag mop stands to one side. Sarah recognizes the cheap white motel towels, now stained ombre from deep red to pale pink and spilling out of a garbage bag. The brothers are wiping down the sofa, wearing respirator masks. The vinyl slipcover gleams. Grandma Sweet had been prescient in her zeal for protecting the upholstery.

The floor and wood panel walls are clean too, the broken pottery and dried grass whisked away, the coffee table straightened. Even the stag's nose has been blotted so the bloodstain looks like a natural discoloration.

Elijah wipes down the antlers with a wet washcloth, almost reverently. The blood on his shirt has dried, and Sarah's not sure if it's his or Ben's. She feels a pang of guilt that she got to have a hot shower while he's walking around with injuries.

"Is there anything I can do?" she asks, setting her smaller bag down next to the towels.

She expects Caleb to say, *You've done enough.* But when he turns to her, the eyes above the mask are kind. "We're almost finished. We just need to take down the curtains. If you want to be useful, you could get his things out of the hall closet. Put on a pair of gloves first."

He motions to the disposable gloves beside the bucket. Sarah pulls the latex over her fingers, feeling like Grandma's plastic-covered couch.

She opens the hall closet and smells Ben's coat before she sees it, even over the whiff of bleach. His particular blend of soap and aftershave and deodorant lingers. So familiar, another intimacy she doesn't want anymore. She viciously yanks the coat and scarf off the hanger. The crisp wool of the coat swings in her hand like a pendulum, weighed down by its pockets' contents.

She draws out a key on a black fob and a phone. Facial recognition probably won't identify Ben's battered and bloodied face, so she can't unlock the phone. Not that she wants to call Graham now anyway. He didn't believe her and had asked Ben to pick her up, and look what happened. Look what he did. What did she do to deserve this?

The key, however, is not the key to the apartment they'd shared, but for a car. The rental car in the driveway. Sarah's heart leaps into her mouth. This is the chance she's been waiting for. She could grab her backpack and run out the door right now. Get in the car and keep driving. Vanish into the blowing snow like so many visitors to the Suicide Motel before her.

A warm, latex-sheathed hand plucks the phone and key out of her palm.

"I'll leave the car at the motel," Caleb says. "That was the pattern with the other disappearances. He came to the house, you rejected him, he went away angry. We'll drop his things in the woods and back you up. Uncle Isaac will believe us. I'll call him in a day or two and report the car, if he doesn't drop by and see it himself."

Caleb holds out another garbage bag, and Sarah drops in the coat and scarf. He rests the phone on top and pockets the key, and then tucks the bag back in the closet.

And just like that, all the remnants of Sarah's old life are stashed away. Yes, it's easy to believe Ben would drive away from the house, his head clouded by rage, then abandon the car and walk into the woods. Drawn by the call many men have heard before him. *Do you hear us screaming? Come, you can scream with us.* Another tithe paid to the Suicide Motel.

Elijah ties up the garbage bags and brings them to Caleb. He takes off his mask and smiles, wincing from the cut on his lip. "Good as new," he says, waving a gloved hand at the gleaming parlor. Sarah could convince herself that Ben never showed up if it wasn't for the coppery tang of his blood on her tongue.

Caleb peels off his own mask and pushes sweat-damp hair off his forehead with the back of his wrist. "I'll move the car and then take these to the town dump. I have to go anyway to toss the broken glass and crap from the motel. No one's going to find that suspicious. Elijah, get your coat."

"He can't go out like that," Sarah says.

Elijah's face is a war zone. Caleb exhales. "You're right. Will you two be okay here alone?"

"Of course," Sarah says. "I'll get him cleaned up."

Caleb nods. "First aid kit is in your bathroom. I'll be back soon. Lock the door."

When the door closes behind him, Sarah turns the deadbolt and snaps into action. She finds an unopened bag of peas in the kitchen freezer, wraps it in a tea towel, and hands it to Elijah. He presses it against his darkening eye. She doesn't want to sit in the parlor ever again, so she says, "Come on," and heads up the stairs.

She leads Elijah to the main bedroom. He hangs back in the doorway, pain in his good eye. "He can't hurt you anymore," she says. But the memory still does, she knows that. She takes his hand and gently guides him across the floor.

The room is warmer than the rest of the house, like it's the heart of Sweetside Manor. It *is* the heart after all, if it had once hosted Jacob Vass. Its dark, rotten heart, beating with ugly secrets. It's appropriate she's sleeping here.

Elijah sits on the bed and picks up the beat-up copy of *Macbeth*. "Who would've thought the old man to have had so much blood in him?" he quotes from behind the bag of frozen peas, his split lip quirking.

Sarah grimaces. "Please don't joke, Elijah."

She finds the first aid supplies and dabs the cuts on Elijah's face with antiseptic ointment. He whimpers, twitching a little, and she remembers how he'd curled up in a ball to deflect Ben's kicks.

"Oh my God. You must be—" Sarah snares the hem of his paint- and blood-spattered shirt and gently tugs it over his head. His torso is lean and pale, a boy's body even though he's not much younger than her. None of the skin is broken, but a mottled red runs up and down his arms and along his ribcage, casting the white lines of old scars in stark relief. His chest rises and falls slowly, his eyes sad as if his mother's ghost is looking out from his face.

Sarah wonders whose ghost looks out from her face.

She touches one blushing rib with a fingertip. "I don't know how to tell if anything's broken."

"They're not. I know what it feels like."

"Oh, Elijah." This sad, lonely boy took the brunt of Ben's anger, and his father's. Her eyes well up with tears, and she puts a hand on his bare shoulder. He leans his cheek against it. His skin is cold from the frozen peas. He smells like blood, but it doesn't turn her stomach anymore.

It smells like freedom.

It smells like being alive.

It smells safe.

She blinks, releasing a tear down her face, and she realizes she's happy.

They sit quietly, Elijah's cold cheek pressing into the back of her hand, listening to their breathing and the call of the wind. A warmth blooms in the pit of her stomach. Not the full-body flush she feels around Caleb, but the coziness of a favorite sweater. Elijah's easy to be around; he wears his feelings on his sleeve. As opposed to Caleb, who shuttles between an easy smile and a smouldering tension in his upper body, as if he's fighting his inheritance of violence. Elijah doesn't seem to want anything in return. He's just glad of the company.

As for what Caleb wants, she doesn't know.

After a minute, she helps Elijah put his shirt back on. "Did you like it?" he asks.

"Like what?"

"Killing Ben."

She laughs nervously. "No, of course not."

"You don't have to lie to me," Elijah says. "I didn't mean if you liked the gory part, but the look of surprise on his face. Did you like that?"

Sarah closes her eyes and remembers that moment. The delicious rawness of her fury. Another tear follows the first, trickling over her upper lip, warm and salty as Ben's blood. "Yes," she whispers. "Yes."

"The moment when you knew he couldn't hurt you anymore."

"Yes." Sarah's voice wobbles with guilt. "I wanted him to get up so I could hit him again. I wanted him to know *I* killed him, that I won and he lost."

He nods as if she's given the right answer.

"Do you wish you'd done the same to your dad?" The question spills out before she can stop it. But she knows he won't be offended. She's killed for him. They're beyond offending each other now.

His eyes stray to the old recliner. He doesn't have to say anything. She understands. The answer is *yes, yes,* and *yes* again.

"I see you," he says softly. "You don't have to pretend anymore. It hurts to pretend, doesn't it?"

He touches her cheek, and the knot she's been holding inside her for so long uncoils, and suddenly she can breathe. *I see you.* He sees her and accepts her.

"Are you sorry?" he asks.

"No," she says, and this time she feels no guilt or shame at the answer. *This* is what freedom really feels like. Not the anxious flight up Highway 11, or the relief at your abuser's death, but the lack of weight on your soul. This is what Ben felt, and what Caleb must feel too, as men moving through the world without having to gauge how much space they take up.

Sarah's face hardens with the truth. "No, I'm not. He should've died the first time."

"Good."

He gifts her his sweet, innocent smile, and for the first time in a long time, Sarah feels at peace.

CHAPTER TWELVE

Elijah lends her a spare hooded sweatshirt, as hers is headed for a trash dump, hopefully never to be unearthed. Caleb returns a couple of hours later with an early dinner, and Sarah realizes they never had lunch. Who can eat, anyway, when there's a body in the garage, waiting to be buried in the spring like a gladiolus bulb. She thinks of Jacob Vass and Stuart McGee and Joseph Singh, lost in the woods and shrouded by snow and dirt and time, their bones planted in the soil and blooming into white pines. Maybe it's the trees that scream, not the wind, with the voices of the disappeared.

Elijah takes a seat at the kitchen table while Caleb lays out an extra-large pepperoni pizza and a Caesar salad. Sarah grabs plates and forks and sits with them. No one says anything. Caleb doesn't even comment on how she knows where everything is in the kitchen. It seems natural, her being there. She's family now. They share everything. If she brought the virus into their house, it's too late, they all have it. If she brought violence, it's made itself at home.

Sarah and Caleb sit on either side of Elijah. He takes both their hands in his. "Let us give thanks," he says, bowing his head. Caleb coughs but says nothing.

Sarah silently thanks the woods for taking Ben, and Elijah releases them.

She bites into a slice and chews tiredly, watching the snowflakes streak past the kitchen window.

"Sarah?" Caleb says.

Both he and Elijah are staring at her. She glances down and realizes tomato sauce is dripping between her fingers, like blood. Caleb hands her a napkin. She takes it, but licks the sauce off her skin instead. There's no need to be polite anymore. Elijah meets her eyes and nods slightly. *I see you.*

Elijah wolfs down the last of his salad and stands up. "I'll be in my studio."

"Elijah, you're in no condition to work. Your face looks worse than the pizza, and I'd hate to see the rest of you." Caleb turns to Sarah. "His ribs?"

Sarah shakes her head.

"Rest, Elijah. Please." Caleb gets up and touches Elijah's shoulder. Elijah looks so small and young, slouching in front of him, as if he's Caleb's son and not his brother. Caleb could crush him easily between his hands, or with just a word.

"I think it's a good idea," Sarah says, and Caleb glances back at her gratefully. "I don't know how you can see anything out of that eye anyway."

Elijah studies the linoleum, his mouth a sullen line. "All right."

Caleb enfolds him in a gentle hug. "I'm glad you're okay. I always am."

"I know." He wriggles out of Caleb's arms like a cat and slips out of the kitchen. The staircase begins to sing his steps.

Sarah starts to collect the dirty dishes, but Caleb waves her away. "You should rest, too. It's been a long day."

"It's been just as long for you."

His smile is weary, but genuine. "Taking care of people is what I do."

Taking care of Elijah, and likely taking care of his father when Jacob Vass's drunken rages petered out. Taking care of the Suicide Motel's customers. And now feeding and sheltering her and helping her bury the body. Sarah drinks in his face for a long second and then reluctantly leaves the kitchen.

She climbs the staircase. The house knows her step now. Soft and harmless, like the face she puts on for people. The floorboards yield gently beneath her socked feet. Elijah's bedroom door is closed. She pauses, feeling the urge to go in and tuck the sheets around him, smooth the hair off his swollen face. But she should let him rest.

In her room, she stretches out on the bed, fidgeting as restlessly as the swaying trees outside. How can Caleb expect her to sleep when Ben is cooling off in the garage? Trying to lie still only encourages her thoughts to run amok. She clambers off the mattress and paces the floor. If her body is busy, her brain can't stop to think, can't run through those last moments with Ben in the parlor.

The house sighs as Caleb climbs the stairs, his footsteps stopping down the hall. A door closes. Pipes rattle as a shower turns on. Water blasting against porcelain drowns out everything else.

Sarah glances out the window above the bed. Dusk has fallen, softly, like a blanket. The wind puts its shoulder against the side of the house, again and again, and she sees Elijah's figure walking into the woods. She recognizes the bulky shoulders of Jacob Vass's shearling coat. The trees part for him, crowning him with their snowy fronds. He is their king. No, only a prince. Jacob Vass is their king. The king of the disappeared. The first to enter the breach from the Suicide Motel.

A soft knock interrupts her thoughts, and Sarah realizes the shower has stopped.

"Do you have a minute?" Caleb says, which is a strange question to ask when she's trapped here with all the time in the world.

She opens the door. Caleb looms over her. He doesn't chide her this time for leaving the door unlocked.

"What is it?" she asks.

Behind him, Elijah's bedroom is still closed. Did she imagine him walking into the woods? Maybe she actually saw Jacob Vass on the day he disappeared. On a snowy night like this, space seems nebulous, irrelevant, and time has no meaning anymore after months in lockdown. Maybe on the night she came to the Suicide Motel, it was Jacob Vass who watched from the window of the house, and the day Caleb first took her to the backyard, it was Jacob's figure behind the plastic of the sunroom. A sentinel for the next person who longed to vanish into the woods.

Caleb runs a hand through his damp curls. "I know the last time I stood here, you weren't happy with me."

The last time he'd stood there seems like many lifetimes ago. He raises his eyes to meet hers, and she forgets why she'd been unhappy. She can't imagine why anyone would be unhappy with someone with eyes as blue as his.

"I accused you of knowing nothing about me and Elijah. But I guess you do understand after all." He wets his lips. "I want to thank you for defending him. He's all I have."

"It was my fault," she blurts, because it's always her fault. "Ben was my—"

"He wasn't your anything. He was his own person, and he chose to attack Elijah. You did what you had to do to save him."

"I'm sure anyone would've done the same."

His smile is faint. "I doubt it. You've spent time with Elijah now. You don't think he's a little—off?"

"I think he's very sweet."

"He is, but he's prone to impulses." Caleb runs his hand through his hair again. "I lied about the knives the other day. We don't have any because I got rid of them. I'm afraid Elijah will hurt himself."

Sarah frowns, trying to remember what Elijah had said about the knives. Surely Caleb was the one with the storm inside him, like their father. Not Elijah.

"I've spent my whole life trying to protect him, and for someone else to come along and also—"

His voice breaks. Sarah says, softly, "Like you would have."

"Like I would have." His eyes darken; bright and clear one moment, a starless sky the next. Outside, the wind crashes against the house, demanding passage.

His gaze seizes hers. She can't look away. His usual easy charm and confidence have evaporated. There's no room for frills in the little space between them. His face is open in a way that's like Elijah but not like Elijah, because Elijah doesn't make her skin burn from head to toe. Elijah doesn't parch the inside of her mouth with want.

"I've been alone for so long," he says.

The blood sings in Sarah's ears again, but this time it's not her fight-or-flight reflex.

She reaches out and touches his cheek.

"So have I," she says.

He's so beautiful, as guileless as Elijah in a lot of ways. His hand flies up to cover hers. He closes his eyes and leans into her, his stubble digging into her palm.

"I see you," she says. "You don't have to pretend anymore." *You don't have to pretend you're holding it all together.* "It hurts to pretend, doesn't it?"

"Yes," he whispers. "Yes."

His voice trembles. Something lurches in Sarah's chest. It's heady, this power. Maybe this was what was missing from her relationship with

Ben. Caleb is a little scared of her, as scared as she is of him. Is this what love is really supposed to feel like? Desire wrapped in fear?

Yesterday she would've told herself to step back and say good night. Today she killed a man. And if she can kill a man, she can love one too, just because she wants to. Because she's finally free.

Sarah slides her fingers down his cheek, tracing the strong line of his jaw until her fingertip rests in the dimple in his chin. He takes her hand and presses his lips to her fingers. At her gasp, he presses another kiss to the heel of her hand, then the tender inside of her wrist, looking at her through long lashes. It is a question.

She answers it by drawing him into the room and closing the door behind him.

"You don't owe me anything," he says. "I'm the one who owes you. Are you sure you want this?"

She turns off the light, drags his head down to hers, and kisses him.

Being intimate with a new partner is a mental battleground. It takes a long time to erase someone from your body. Caleb's smell is different. His weight is different. The shape of his body, the way he moves, the noises he makes, his touch—warm and unhurried, almost reverential, like he can't believe she's real—it's all different, but it's not enough to escape the muscle memory of the past eight years. Sarah moves with him, screwing her eyes shut as if she can evict the image of Ben's face. With every stroke, the voice at the back of her head whispers, *Ben, Ben, Ben,* even though he's dead.

She grabs Caleb's hips, terrified of moaning the wrong name, and meets his thrusts with a determination fueled by passion and fear. She opens her eyes and watches his face, wondering if he's remembering a past lover, too. Each grimace as he strains—is it for her, or for the memory of another woman? Is it desire, or dread?

It is a terrible thing to close your eyes to pleasure and find someone unwanted waiting there, like a ghost standing in the middle of your dream house.

Afterward, she snuggles in his arms, her limbs soft and heavy, careful to lie on the side of the bed opposite to where she used to sleep with Ben. The difference is enough to be a relief. And Caleb is bigger than Ben, more solid.

"You're beautiful," she murmurs, skimming his chest with the flat of her hand, tracing faded scars that match Elijah's. His fingers tense briefly around her shoulder. She's said the wrong thing, even if it's true. She forgot he owes his physique to his father, to the threat of violence. A ghost haunting his body, as Ben haunts hers.

He presses his lips to her temple and says, "So are you," and she knows she's forgiven.

But he can't be right. She's not beautiful, because just as Jacob Vass shaped his eldest son, Ben has shaped her. What will she become because of him?

Her last thought as she drifts into sleep is that she came all this way to escape Ben, but there might be no escape after all.

Sarah wakes a few hours later and untangles herself from Caleb's sleeping form. The windows glow a deep indigo-grey, providing enough light for her to groggily stumble to the bathroom. When she returns, she catches a glint of metal on the floor.

A handful of keys splay from a carabiner, attached to Caleb's discarded jeans.

She jolts to full alertness. She could grab her backpack, get into his truck, and drive away from Sweetside. Disappear into the night and finally start the new life for which she's been longing for months.

She crouches over the puddle of clothes and reaches for the carabiner, her insides trembling.

"What are you doing?" Caleb's tousled head rises from the pillows.

Sarah smiles at him. "I was just picking the clothes off the floor." She scoops them up and deposits them on the recliner. "What did you think I was doing?" she adds, letting an accusatory note slip into her voice.

It's something Ben would say.

"I'm sorry," says Caleb. "Come back to bed."

As she burrows into his arms, the thing that's been nagging her all evening finally puts itself into words. "Caleb," she whispers, "why would you think Elijah killed Ben?" Elijah is so sweet, so vulnerable, and Caleb normally treats him like a child. It doesn't make sense.

Caleb's reply is a murmur; he's falling back asleep.

Of course he'd assume Elijah had done it. She's the nice girl in need of rescuing, utterly harmless.

Her last thought before sleep overtakes her is that maybe she should lock the door.

She doesn't know what time it is when she opens her eyes and sees Elijah standing at the foot of the bed. "What is it?" she wants to say, but her mouth refuses to open. She's curled up and frozen stiff, like Ben in his salt-filled coffin, weight pressing against her from all directions. If she opens her mouth, it'll fill with salt.

She can't make out his face, only the boxy silhouette of the shearling coat. Maybe there isn't anyone wearing it. Or maybe there is, but it's not Elijah. She expects the apparition to growl *Someone's been sleeping in my bed,* but he remains silent. She grunts, trying to remember if she locked the door. Why didn't she lock the door? Caleb always told her to. Or was it Elijah? She can't keep track of who said what anymore.

The howling wind lets up. It's not her pulse stuttering, but an engine outside. Is Ben pulling up to the house? Is he finally home? Will he come into the room and slip into bed beside her, or go to sleep on the sofa? The freshly cleaned and sterilized sofa? She grunts again but still can't move.

The apparition in the shearling coat tilts its head toward the window, listening. *Ben's coming,* she wants to yell. *Get away, Elijah. He's coming.*

Broken glass tinkles in the distance. Terror curdles on her tongue. She's huddled in the bathroom at the Suicide Motel, the floor tiles cold and hard under her bare feet, shoulder blades digging into the door.

The weight pressing against her back stirs. It's only Caleb. The wave of terror breaks, and her eyes pop open.

"Elijah," she croaks.

It's too late. The figure has disappeared, leaving behind the scent of tobacco and turpentine.

CHAPTER THIRTEEN

Sarah is alone when sunlight breaks through the front windows, rousing her from sleep. For once, it's not snowing, but the sky is the color of an old soup bone. She stretches in the enormous bed, disappointed there's no sign of Caleb except the scent left on the sheets. He smells like soap and fabric softener, simple masculine scents. Unlike Elijah's cedar-and-turpentine or the faded tobacco Jacob Vass left behind. Or the metallic tang of Ben's blood.

She rescues her abandoned pajama top and pads to the bathroom. When she comes out, there's a knock on the door. She was afraid it would be awkward but no, Caleb grins down at her holding a tray, this time carrying breakfast for two. They drink coffee and eat muffins together in his father's bed, her bare legs hooked over his. After staring death in the face, this feels so easy. It's always easy, at the beginning, she reminds herself. But she pushes the thought away as Caleb kisses her neck. She's unbuttoning his jeans when his cell phone rattles against his hip.

He groans and takes it out of his pocket. "Shit," he says, glancing at the screen. "It's Uncle Isaac."

The name sends a bucket of ice water over Sarah's skin. Caleb rolls away and strides to the other side of the room. Sarah clamps a hand over her mouth and tries not to giggle, tries not to even breathe for fear of setting the bedsprings squeaking. Isaac can't know she's been considerably less than six feet apart from Caleb.

"Uh huh?" Caleb raises his eyebrows. "Both families? Okay. I need to stop at Murry's for more plywood. See you as soon as I can."

He hangs up and rubs the back of his neck. "Shit. I'm sorry. I have to go right away. I can't give Uncle Isaac an excuse to swing by looking for me."

He's right. The moment is ruined, anyway. He shrugs his shirt back on and hurriedly buttons it up. "I'll be back for dinner," he says, leaning over the bed to kiss her.

She gets dressed, and then brings the dirty dishes down to the kitchen. Elijah wanders downstairs a little later, and she brews another pot of coffee and sits with him in his studio. It's all very cozy and domestic.

If he had come into the main bedroom the night before, he says nothing. He doesn't mention her newfound intimacy with Caleb, and neither does she. He seems pleased to have her attention, and to answer her questions about his painting. Probably no one has ever shown this much interest in his work, not even Caleb, who would've been too busy at the motel all day to offer anything more than vague compliments.

Sarah curls up on the loveseat with a book, occasionally glancing up to admire Elijah's progress. Thick brushstrokes drag down the canvas, wet and gleaming and reeking of linseed oil. Her head swims at the smell and vision. The impression is of black pines at night, bleeding from their branches. This is what Elijah sees when he walks in the woods, and when he looks through the layers of plastic that should have been the sunroom's back windows.

This is what Sarah sees too when she looks out at the woods, what Jacob Vass and the other men must have seen. *Do you hear the screaming?*

Elijah moves stiffly, although his eye looks less puffy today. Sarah doesn't want to let him out of her sight. She saved his life, and now she feels responsible for him. Caleb may have gotten rid of all the knives, but maybe one day Elijah will go into the woods and never come back, as his father did before him.

After lunch, the book slips from her hand, and the comforting scent of turpentine and cedar lulls her to sleep on the loveseat.

She's woken by a light touch on her hand. The sky has dimmed, and Elijah has turned on a floodlight. She stirs and discovers Jacob Vass's shearling coat tucked around her. It's warm and heavy and smells faintly of tobacco.

Caleb crouches beside her, hair falling over his face. Her heart lurches at how humbled and weary he appears. He didn't have time to shave today, and the stubble only emphasizes the deep planes of his face.

"Hi," he says. He glances at Elijah, who's mixing yet another shade of black. Elijah doesn't seem to notice him, nor the frown that briefly creases his brow. "Want to help me with dinner?"

Sarah pushes the coat off and he helps her up. She follows him into the kitchen, her hand swallowed in his. There's a slight tug in his grip, a sense of urgency she doesn't quite understand, but she's touched he wants to get her alone after a hard day.

Caleb browns the ground beef, and she puts a pot of water on the stovetop to boil for pasta. Like the morning, it's all very comfortable, like they've been cooking together for years. His smile doesn't reach his eyes, though, and there's a tension in his shoulders that wasn't there earlier. She wonders if Isaac said something to remind him she's supposed to be in quarantine, not laughing with him in the kitchen, playfully flinging strands of cooked spaghetti at each other.

"Is anything wrong?" she finally asks.

Caleb stops stirring the sauce and slumps against the counter. "This morning when I left, there were a couple of broken beer bottles on the porch."

Sarah remembers the car engine she thought she'd heard last night, the clink of glass. A chill creeps across her skin, and she wishes she was wearing the shearling coat again.

"Then I went to Murry's Hardware, and they wouldn't talk to me. I mean, I get side-eye at the best of times, but they refused to serve me. I had to call Uncle Isaac to come and persuade them."

"But why?" Sarah asks, although she knows.

"They know you're staying here. They think I might have the virus, too."

Sarah's blood runs to ice water. "Oh God. I'm sorry." It's her fault, it's always her fault. She's brought this on their house. Opened a door and let all the hatred in. She doesn't belong, as much as she fooled herself into thinking she did.

He shakes his head. "Nothing for you to be sorry about."

Sarah sets out the plates, her mind and stomach roiling. Time is ticking by. How many days has she been here? Too many.

She could stay here, she knows. Tangled up with Caleb at night, playing house with Elijah during the day. While the wolves outside howl for her blood and the virus closes in. But it's another prison, like the one she'd inhabited with Ben. He whispers in her ear now, with the wind. *What did I do to deserve this?*

He's never far from her thoughts. Literally. The knowledge that his body is just in the garage haunts her. She can't pass the parlor without replaying how he'd sprayed blood in her mouth, which seems more intimate and violating than any sexual relations they'd had together. He's tainted Sweetside Manor with his memory. She might as well still be trapped with him.

He wins.

She has to leave before she runs out of choices. If she stays here, she'll never know who she is without Ben.

You already know who you are, Ben whispers in her head.

Caleb's truck is the only way out. Sarah ambles to a drawer and pulls out three forks and spoons, all of which are tarnished. Everything in this cursed house is old or dead.

"Come away with me," she says, turning to Caleb.

"What?"

"Come away with me. The motel's closed, there's nothing for you here. We could pack our stuff tonight and get in your truck and go."

He laughs. "Go where?"

"Anywhere. I've got my laptop, I have a roster of clients. All I need is wifi. I can work anywhere. Even in a parking lot outside a coffee shop if I have to. We could get on the Trans-Canada Highway and find someplace new to put down roots."

He shakes his head. "It's a nice dream, but I don't think so. What am I going to do for work? And during a pandemic?"

"You said you don't really need to work."

"That doesn't mean I don't want to. A man likes to be useful."

She pictures him hammering boards over a window, the inhabitants inside spitting or swearing or begging for mercy. She swallows. "You managed a motel for most of your adult life. That's good for something. You're smart, Caleb. You'll figure out how to survive outside Sweetside."

"What about Elijah?"

The more she thinks about it, the more excited she gets. There's no reason to stay in this tiny, insular town where they're all outcasts. "He'll come with us. We could go somewhere and start fresh, where no one knows us. Where no one cares what I look like. Board up the house, or sell it, or give the keys to your uncle, whatever. We could disappear and leave this all behind."

He shakes his head again, dousing her hope. "I can't— Elijah can't leave this house. You don't understand."

Sarah slams the silverware down on the table. She feels it now. The storm brewing inside her. The wind whispers in her ear. *Yes. Let it out. It feels good to show your anger, doesn't it?*

"This fucking house, the motel, Elijah—they're holding you back," she snaps.

"I can't leave Elijah." His eyes are pleading, and Sarah hates herself for causing him distress. But at the same time, a perverse pride blazes in her chest that she's capable of such cruelty.

She gestures in the direction of the sunroom. "I care about Elijah, too! But it's not healthy how much you hover over him. He's a grown man; he's got to learn how to stand on his own two feet. And so do you."

"He's all I have. He's family." Caleb picks up a spoon and returns to the sauce.

Sarah puts her hand on his, stopping him from stirring.

"I could be your family, too."

His eyes meet hers for a single heart-stopping second.

"But obviously you don't care enough about me to even talk about it," she says.

She releases his hand and stalks out of the kitchen. "Aren't you going to have dinner?" Caleb calls out.

"I'm not hungry."

She *is* hungry. Very hungry. But she continues stomping up the staircase. She wants to hurt the house. She wants to hurt Caleb. She wants to leave bruises.

She flounces into her room and locks the door behind her. Crossing her arms, she glares out the window above the bed. Elijah is hurrying across the backyard toward the woods. He sees her, and waves happily. Her face softens and she waves back. Elijah would leave Sweetside with her without hesitation, if she asked.

About five minutes later, the stairs creak. Caleb's footsteps, no longer so confident.

He raps on the door. "Sarah?"

She says nothing, only prickles with irritation while watching the spot where Elijah disappeared.

"Sarah, please." Caleb jiggles the doorknob. "Don't be mad. I'm sorry. It's just a lot to think about."

She still doesn't answer, imagining him running a hand through his overgrown curls, frown lines marring his forehead.

Finally he says the magic words. The words that ran through her head whenever Ben picked a fight with her.

"What did I do wrong?" he says. "How can we go back to where we were?"

It takes Sarah's breath away how easy it is to have power over someone. *You already know who you are*, Ben whispers again.

Sarah unlocks and opens the door. Caleb's face slackens with relief. She's careful to keep her expression neutral. She's had a lot of practice.

"I don't belong in Sweetside, and neither do you," she says.

"You're wrong about that. I do belong here."

"You don't. I wish you'd see that."

He gently places his hands on her upper arms. "We can talk about it later. Don't get me wrong, Sarah. It's not that I don't want to be with you. I like you a lot. I want you to be happy. You deserve to be happy."

Like herself, he's spent his life trying to please others. His father, his uncle, Elijah, even the townspeople who treat him like a pariah. But she can't let him see she sympathizes, not when he's eating out of her hand.

"For now, can you please come down for dinner?" he begs.

Sarah lowers her eyes, her jaw set. But she says, "Okay," and he smiles as if he's won a major victory when it's really her who's won.

Sarah follows him down the stairs and back to the kitchen, where she resumes setting the table. "I'll get Elijah," Caleb says, heading for the sunroom before she can tell him she saw Elijah outside.

The front door squeaks open, and she hears Elijah stomping the snow off his boots on the doormat. She goes to meet him. If she tells him she wants to leave, maybe he can convince Caleb it's the right thing to do.

Elijah clutches a long, pale object. "I dug this up in the woods," he says proudly.

"Elijah, *no!*" Caleb roars, storming down the hall.

Sarah startles, and Elijah freezes like a deer in headlights. "It's just a branch," he says in a small voice. He looks pathetic with his black eye and scarred lip. "All the bark got stripped off, so it looks like a bone. I thought it was cool. I wanted to show Sarah."

Caleb sags against the staircase bannister, and the tension in Sarah's body eases. He's not turning into Jacob Vass. Yet. "Fuck. I'm sorry, Elijah. I didn't mean to yell like that. I thought you were going to show her something gross. Go wash up for dinner."

Elijah sets the branch on the side table and retreats into the downstairs bathroom to wash his hands.

Caleb gives a shaky laugh. "He's always digging stuff up in the woods. The last time I had a girl over for dinner, he dragged in a rotting squirrel head. He was so proud of it, too. That didn't help our reputation as the town weirdos." He pinches the spot between his eyes. "I hate it when I yell at Elijah. But sometimes it just comes out."

He lifts his head to meet Sarah's gaze. "Do you ever feel like you're becoming someone you hate?"

It's so easy to lie. Why didn't she figure this out before? So easy to swear that up is down and black is white. She learned from the best, after all.

Sarah smiles. "No, never."

CHAPTER FOURTEEN

Sarah lies that night in Caleb's arms again, him wrapped around her as if she could slip away at any moment. He doesn't talk to her about leaving, as he'd promised, only touches her as if he can convince her to stay with the ferocity of his adoration.

This time she remembers to lock the door.

Before she falls asleep, she realizes the keys are missing from his pants, as if he's intentionally hidden them from her.

At dawn she wakes to a dead weight slung over her body. Panic sweeps through her as she tries to struggle free. "Where do you think you're going?" a male voice growls. A beefy arm tightens around her waist. It's Jacob Vass, reclaiming his place in the bed.

She kicks and Caleb says, "Hey, hey, easy there," and she remembers she's safe. For now. Though she might as well be in bed with his father, the way the storm crashes inside him, trying to batter its way out.

"I have to pee," she says, and he releases her, laughing, his fingers scraping her bare back as she wriggles away. Tracing the invisible target between her shoulder blades.

When she returns to bed, he kisses that spot, reminding her it can never be taken off. She shivers. Caleb's arms constrict around her, assuming she'd shivered out of pleasure and not dread.

Sleep doesn't return to either of them, and after a slow, unhurried tangling of breath and limbs, Caleb climbs out of bed with a grunt.

She admires the broadness of his shoulders as he stretches, the muscles shifting across his back. He doesn't have a target there. "I have to go into town again. I need to pick up some things before the grocery store gets busy," he says.

She sits up and pulls the quilt up under her arms. "Are you going to be okay?"

"I don't know."

She bites her lip, partly from concern, partly from resentment. *He can drive through town, and no one will shoot at him like they tried to shoot Graham. The worse they'll do is refuse to serve him, like yesterday.* "I'm sure you'll be fine," she says petulantly.

"I can ask about the garage again if you like, but they'll still be closed."

"Sure," she says, hugging her knees. "Whatever."

"Don't be mad. Please. Can you blame me if I want you to stay a little longer?"

"You said you want me to be happy, but you don't care about what I need."

"That's not true."

"I need to get out of Sweetside. It's not safe for me. It's barely safe for *you* now. They're coming to the house. How long until they break your windows? Break down the door?"

"Uncle Isaac won't let them do that," he says, and Sarah scoffs, because where was Isaac when she was alone at the motel? "We need to ride out the rest of your quarantine, and then we can see about getting your car. Or I'll drive you to Timmins myself to your brother's place."

"Graham's the last person I want to see now," she mutters. "God, it's your dad."

Caleb stiffens. "What about my dad?"

"It's like his spirit is hanging around here. All the hatred and violence and suspicion. Can't you feel it?"

He fits the profile, Elijah had said. She sees it clearly now, illuminated by the morning light. The breadth of his shoulders, the unapologetic way he cuts through a space. The way his anger uses up all the air in the room so there's none left for her to breathe.

"Haven't you heard the screaming in the woods? Haven't you heard it calling to you?" Because *she* has, every day.

Caleb sinks to the bed. Bows his head like he's praying to her. "Yes," he whispers.

All the times she thought she saw Jacob Vass, as if he were an omen,

Caleb had been nearby. What if his father's ghost is actually watching *him*, not her? Waiting to lead him into the woods?

"Then why can't you take me away from here?"

"I can't, Sarah."

Her anger flares. How can he be so stubborn? "Give me one good reason. A real reason, not an excuse. And nothing to do with Elijah."

Caleb lifts his eyes to hers, and for once, she can't read his expression.

"Someone has to bury Ben in the spring," he says.

Hopeless fury squeezes her lungs like a fist. It's not Caleb's blindness to the danger, or even Jacob Vass's presence, but Ben who still has a hold on her.

"I have to go." Caleb slides off the bed and leaves the room without looking back.

When the truck drives away, Sarah buries her face into a pillow and screams. No one can hear you scream out here, after all.

As Sarah gets dressed, the stairs squeak in Elijah's rhythm. Her resolve quickens. If Caleb won't help her, Elijah will. He's like a puppy. He brought her that branch yesterday, hoping for a pat on the head. Ever since she saved him from Ben, he looks at her differently.

She follows the scent of coffee down to the kitchen. Elijah leans against the counter, shovelling cereal into his mouth while the coffee percolates.

"Good morning. Your face looks better," she says. Most of the swelling has gone down, and the cut on his lip is almost a memory.

"I feel better, too," he says, but she winces, thinking of the bruises across his arms and torso. Her own bracelet is fading around the edges to a jaundiced shade of yellow.

She helps herself to a blueberry muffin from the tray on the counter and leans beside him, her shoulder pressing companionably against his. "What are you up to today?" she asks, although she knows the answer. More painting, maybe a walk in the woods. She's not sure how he can stand to do the same thing day after day, but probably when you're an artist, every day is full of possibilities. And the woods—

The woods are full of possibilities, too. So many vanished men. Has Elijah heard them screaming yet?

"I'm going to drink this coffee," he announces over a mouthful of cereal, "and then I'm going into the woods to drop Ben's things."

Sarah's breath catches, hope igniting like a rocket. The key to Ben's rental car might be available. She could get in and go. Caleb and Elijah could tell Isaac that yes, Ben had stopped there, but the curse of the Suicide Motel had gotten him, and then that Chinese girl had broken quarantine and driven away. Or maybe the Suicide Motel had gotten to her, too.

Half the time, Sarah's not sure if it actually has gotten to her.

"Can I come?" she asks.

He frowns, momentarily resembling Caleb more than either of his parents. "You shouldn't go outside in case Uncle Isaac comes again."

"Caleb went to meet him this morning. We should be good for a bit." So easy to lie to get what you want. *You see why I did it?* Ben whispers in the back of her head. She puts on an eager smile. "I'd like to see the woods. I haven't been in them yet."

Elijah grins back. She's played her cards correctly. He's thrilled to show her his favorite haunt. "All right then. We'll go out the back in case someone sees you."

They gather up their outdoor things. Elijah leads her through the house, pulling on a pair of latex gloves. He picks up the garbage bag puddled by his easel, and then they head out the sunroom's side door.

Sarah hasn't been outside since the day Graham was supposed to pick her up, and the morning chill is an unforgiving slap to her cheeks. The wind tousles her hair and drags it across her face like a veil. She shoves her hands into her pockets, regretting she didn't ask to borrow a pair of mittens.

"This way," Elijah says. He doesn't need to tell her. The gap in the woods yawns up ahead, the path smoothed over from the previous night's snowfall. The snow is soft, and it yields like flesh to the press of their boots. The pines stretch up to the sky like so many church spires.

The pines had simply looked tall from Sarah's bedroom window. Now, standing at their base, they are colossal. The top boughs sag like collapsed umbrellas under the weight of snow, and at eye level, the branches are bare and broken. Sarah feels like she's underground. Below the surface of the earth, where the bones of the trees have taken root.

From a distance, driving by in the safety of her car, the forests she'd passed had been postcard-perfect landscapes. Within their depths, however, it's all scraggly, amputated branches, bark peeling like hangnails. A harsh gauntlet between naked shrubs and brittle saplings. So many broken, half-dead things to reach out and scratch you. Sarah glances back at the house, but can't see it. It doesn't matter. Branches creak like bowing floorboards. In a way, they're still inside Sweetside Manor. There is no leaving.

"Caleb figures we should scatter Ben's things deep in the woods," Elijah says, his breath swelling into clouds. "That's all they ever found of the others. Just a wallet or a hat."

"Did they ever find anything of your dad's?"

"Just this coat."

Sarah touches his sleeve. The sheepskin feels cool and slippery, like Elijah's own skin. "I'm sorry you don't know for sure if he's gone. That must be scary, the thought he could return any minute."

But he's already here, Ben whispers in her head. Sarah silently tells him to shut up. He can't talk to her; he's dead.

"In a lot of ways, he never left," Elijah says, and Sarah knows he's right.

"What about our footprints?"

"It's going to snow again soon." He squints up at what little of the marrow-grey sky they can see. "And everyone knows I walk through here all the time, and you're wearing my old boots."

He hops over a fallen log, and then takes Sarah's hand and helps her over it. The latex gloves feel cold and clammy against her bare skin. Is this how Ben's bloodless flesh felt as they rolled his body up in the dropsheet? She shoves her hands back into her pockets to ward off the chill, but it's too late. The chill is inside her, tensing her shoulders until they're as stiff and huddled as Ben's corpse.

"If you were really upset, maybe even hallucinating, what would you drop first?" Elijah asks.

Sarah imagines herself finally answering the call of the woods. Stumbling between the trees with nothing but the yearning to disappear.

The wind circles the canopy, making the branches sing. "The phone," she says. "Because fuck the outside world and everyone in it."

Yes. Rage first. Always rage first. That initial flame, kindled in your body before it snuffs out into misery. Sarah thinks of her own dead phone, tucked in her backpack. She hasn't missed it at all. Because fuck everyone outside her little bubble. She called Graham, and look what happened.

Elijah takes out the phone. The battery's at five percent. Ben was always forgetting to charge it, or so he claimed whenever Sarah couldn't reach him. The screen displays a notification for a missed call from Graham. She could try to call him back, but what would she say? That she's calling from a dead man's phone? Anyway, Graham had sent Ben to claim her, as if she were a shopping bag forgotten in a coat check. It's really his fault Ben died.

Rage first. Sarah lifts her chin. "Throw it. Throw it as far as you can."

Elijah hurls it with surprising veracity. It whistles through the air until it strikes a tree trunk and plummets into a nest of snow and fallen branches. Just a thing, in the end, like the Ben-shaped body stiffening in the garage.

"What next?" Elijah asks.

"The scarf." Because you're boiling with fury and disbelief at how your life has gone. The scarf itches, burns, strangles. You plow deeper into the woods and you're too hot and you tear it off and toss it aside. You'll show them. They'll be sorry.

Sarah fiddles with the neck of her borrowed parka, unzipping the suddenly too-tight collar. "Just drop it," she says.

Elijah pulls out the scarf and lets it slip to the ground. She'd bought Ben that scarf last Christmas, because he'd lost his. It's a nice scarf, from the same expensive store where he got his coat, and she bets he told people he'd bought it himself.

"The coat," she says, unzipping her parka all the way.

It's still too hot, even without the scarf. You're burning up. You want to make it stop. You want to make all this *feeling* stop. You want to burrow deeper into the woods until it devours you.

You want to disappear.

Elijah takes out the coat. Dark grey wool, carefully lint brushed before every outing, the lapels sharp and crisp. Appearances had always been important to Ben. No one could know he was a failure, that he hadn't been able to pay off his credit card bill for months after he'd bought that coat.

"Hang it over a branch. Neatly," Sarah says. Even in Ben's state of mind, he wouldn't leave that coat crumpled in the snow. He'd treated it with more care than he'd treated her.

Elijah smooths it over the closest branch. Sarah nods in approval.

The garbage bag wilts in Elijah's hand, shiny and black against the dull paleness of the forest floor. "What's left?" she asks, praying that things go her way for once.

Elijah takes out a single key attached to a fob.

Her heart stops.

"Should I toss this as well?" he asks, crumpling the garbage bag into his coat pocket.

"No!"

She reaches for the key, but Elijah pulls it back. "You're not wearing gloves."

"Ben's car. I don't have to take Caleb's truck. I could take the car to get out of here."

Elijah shakes his head. "Caleb won't like that."

"Fuck what Caleb likes." *Rage first.*

Elijah says nothing, only stubbornly presses his lips together. She takes a deep breath. What would Ben do? Make them feel sorry for you. "Elijah. Help me get out of here. Please. I know I'm supposed to be in quarantine at least another week, but we don't have the time. Caleb says they're turning on him in town. It's because I'm here. It'll be safer for all of us if I go." She doesn't have to fake the tears welling in her eyes.

Elijah closes his fingers over the key. "I can't disobey Caleb. He's family. He's all I have."

Sarah takes a step toward him. What next? Give the love and acceptance they hunger for. Give it and take it away when they don't do what you want.

Now you get it, Ben whispers. *Now you understand.*

"Elijah," She closes a hand over his arm, the arm that holds the key to her freedom. Literally. "I could be your family, too."

Elijah raises his hand like he's about to drop the key into her palm, but then withdraws it. "Take me with you," he says, his Adam's apple bobbing. He's so heartbreakingly young. In Jacob Vass's shearling coat, he looks like a little boy playing dress-up in his father's clothes. "I don't want to be left alone with Caleb. You know how he is. The storm inside him— it's gotten worse lately."

Do you ever feel like you're becoming someone you hate? Jacob Vass hangs over the house like a stench. Elijah was worried one day his father would come back, but Jacob already haunts Sweetside Manor.

"I feel bad leaving him, though. I'm the only one who really understands him," Elijah says. "And I can't help thinking he's right I'm better off at home."

Sarah stares despondently at the paint-stained fist in which the key has disappeared. "That's what he wants you to think. You're smart, Elijah. You'll figure out how to survive outside Sweetside. And I'll look after you," she adds, and she means it. She's already Wendy to his Lost Boy.

"Will you?" He turns his dark, soulful eyes on her. "I've been alone for so long."

Sarah tucks a curl behind his ear. "So have I," she whispers.

She brushes the spot below his black eye gently with her knuckles. His breath trembles. Closing her eyes, she presses her forehead to his. She cups the back of his neck, and he does the same to her, his latex gloves cool and soothing on her skin.

It feels right, to be twinned like this. They're two peas in a pod, her and Elijah. Both damaged. But both survivors.

Sarah's eyes fly open as a metallic jingle interrupts the quiet moment. "Oh, I dropped the key," Elijah says.

Sarah pulls away from him and starts scrabbling in the snow. She has to find the key first. She's happy to take Elijah with her, but she's worried he might withdraw his help if he's afraid of Caleb.

"Got it," Elijah says.

Sarah hides her disappointment with a smile, and then a silver glint beyond his shoulder catches her eye. Another key? Another relic of a disappeared man?

"What is that?" She rambles off the path toward the base of a tree. The roots are exposed like veins, the snow mixed with dirt and dead weeds, as if a wild animal—or Elijah—has been digging.

"It's okay, Sarah. I got it," Elijah says.

Sarah ignores him, crouching over the little metallic knot shining from the overturned dirt.

She brushes away the snow—and rocks back on her heels.

It's a tooth, capped with a crown.

She wipes more of the snow and dirt away and her bare fingers trace a curved row of teeth in a bone the color of the grey sky.

A human jawbone, wide and raw. Like Caleb's.

"It's interesting what you find in the woods," Elijah says.

Sarah straightens, slowly, too numb and bewildered by this discovery to say anything but his name. "Elijah?"

Elijah looks wistfully at the jawbone. "I think a lot about how it must've felt to stab Dad over and over again. To watch him bleed out. To stand over him and let him know who's more powerful. To stand there and know you're alive and he's not."

Sarah's legs lock into place. "Elijah, what are you saying?"

Ben laughs in her head. *You know what he's saying, you stupid girl. You really can pick 'em.*

Elijah's smile is sad and apologetic. "This is why we don't have knives."

Sarah stares down at the bone. Jacob Vass's jawbone, gaping like the photo in the dining room, broken open so he'll always be screaming.

The ease with which Caleb took care of the mess after Ben died makes sense now. And afterward she'd lain in the arms of a killer—

He lay in your arms, killer, whispers Ben.

The revelation hits like a wave of nausea. Sarah's legs give way and grabs a tree to steady herself. The bark nips at her palms, but she barely feels it. "I can't believe—"

"You've spent a lot of time with him now. You don't think he's a little —off?"

Elijah's words echo inside her head, and she gets the nagging feeling she's heard them before. She can't remember who said them. It might have even been her. But it doesn't matter. She just has to get into Ben's car and drive away. She'll sort it out later.

"That night, when you and Caleb—" Elijah blushes. "I came into your room because I was afraid for you. I think you woke up and saw me."

"What about the others? Stuart McGee and Joseph Singh?" Sarah asks, although she knows the answer.

"They're buried here too. *You* understand. That feeling, to stand over someone and feel alive—it's addicting."

Sarah nods, or shudders. *Fight or flight,* her body screams. It's definitely time for flight.

Running away and leaving your mess behind again? Ben whispers.

Sarah staggers in the direction from which they came, breath rattling in her lungs. Elijah follows. "Did you like the story about the screaming in the woods? I thought of it. Some of our guests really have complained about the sound of the wind," he says.

Sarah stumbles again. Bare branches like Elijah's pale fingers snag on her coat, her hair. Pulling her in, demanding that she stay. There were never ghosts screaming from the woods. It was all in her head. Or maybe they were screaming for different reasons. They were crying a warning, not an invitation.

She doesn't know what's true anymore. Black is white, up is down. She might as well still be living with Ben. Her pulse booms, the only constant in her life, the only thing she can be sure of. Her internal compass spins and spins until it points to the only exit.

"Elijah," Sarah rasps. "Let's get out of here."

CHAPTER FIFTEEN

The first thing Sarah grabs when she returns to the house is her knife. Now *the* knife, the only one in the house. It's at the bottom of her backpack, wrapped in the cheap washcloth. She digs it out and shakes off the cloth, dazed by Elijah's bombshell.

Caleb murdered his father. Maybe it had been in self-defense, maybe it was to protect Elijah. Like she'd done to Ben, but Caleb grew a taste for it, and two other men fell to his appetite. An appetite for standing over someone and feeling alive. Feeling free at last.

You know how it feels, Ben whispers.

Sarah tells him to shut up. Her parka is still open, and she slides the knife carefully into the kangaroo pocket of her hoodie.

At least I never killed anyone, Ben whispers.

The second thing Sarah grabs is her backpack. She meets Elijah in the hallway. He holds a full duffel bag, and she wonders if, like herself, he's had that bag packed for months in case he ever needs to run.

You like to run, don't you, Ben whispers.

The staircase whines one last protest as they run down the steps. But Sarah has nothing to fear from the noise now. In the end, Sweetside Manor is only a house, not a living thing, and in time it'll crumble into dust like the bones buried in the woods.

Elijah opens the front door. "Let's go."

Sarah nods grimly. Elijah's not the brother she'd imagined running away with, but Caleb isn't who she thought he was. *No one is ever who you think they are,* Ben whispers. *Not even yourself.*

They hurry down the driveway, boots scraping against salt and gravel and half-melted ice. Sarah's stomach twists as she realizes the fresh salt under their feet could be shoveled from Ben's resting place.

"Shit," Elijah says.

It's the first time she's ever heard him swear.

A red pickup truck rumbles up the road from the motel to the driveway. The horn honks once, twice, the sound ripping through her tightening chest. Elijah grabs her hand. "Come on."

He half-drags her past the truck. Caleb's eyebrows draw together from his seat high up in the cab. The truck screeches to a halt, and the driver-side door swings open.

"Go!" Elijah says.

"Sarah!" Caleb calls out. "What are you doing?"

Elijah's hand squeezes her clammy one. "Don't answer him. Keep heading for the motel."

Sarah runs, her body nothing but swinging arms and legs and stabbing breaths. The truck's motor switches off, and Caleb launches himself out of the driver's seat. "Sarah!" he yells.

"*Run!*" Elijah says, releasing her hand and picking up his heels.

Sarah tries to run faster, but she flails in the too-large boots. Her heart throbs in her throat, and she makes the mistake of glancing back. Caleb sprints toward her, the storm in his eyes as he closes the distance with his powerful legs. He never did have to think about how much space he takes up.

Her mouth opens, ready to scream, anticipating those large, heavy hands around her neck.

He pushes past her and punches Elijah in the face.

Elijah grunts and falls backward onto the snow, dropping the duffel bag. Blood streams from both nostrils.

"Elijah!" Sarah rushes over to him. The key, the precious car key. Is he still holding it?

Elijah's fingers fall open, revealing the black fob.

"Sarah, get away from him!" Caleb roars.

Sarah snatches at the fob, but Elijah's fingers close like a trap. "Help me stand," he hisses.

She glances up. Caleb advances.

"I'm sorry," she whispers, and she stomps on his hand.

To give love and then take it away, that is the only way to stay on top. Elijah yelps and his hand springs open again. Sarah snatches the key and jams it into her pocket.

Elijah spits out a mouthful of blood, scarlet on the white snow. Sarah expects him to say, *What did I do wrong? How can we go back to where we were?*

Instead he starts to laugh, like he did the day Ben hit him. His shoulders shake as he rocks on the snow. "How does it feel? How does it feel to hurt me? Do you feel alive?"

She can't tell if he's talking to her or Caleb.

Caleb stands in her path, as large as a wall. "What did he tell you?" he demands.

She can't think fast enough to lie. "Your dad," she says, her eyes darting around Caleb's body for an exit. "The men who disappeared."

"He told you I killed them."

Her heart is hammering too quickly to choke out an answer.

"It wasn't me, Sarah," Caleb says. "It's him, it's always been him. You have to believe me."

"Of course you'd say that."

"And of course he'd say *I* did it." Caleb thrusts a finger toward his brother. "What did he offer you, to get you to take him with you?"

Sarah's heart slams so hard and fast against her ribs, she can't hear anything else Caleb says. His mouth moves but she doesn't understand the words. *Make them feel sorry for you, then give love and acceptance.* Was Elijah playing her all along as she played him, and Caleb? Showing her a harmless, innocent face, so that she would trust him instantly.

They're more alike than she thought.

You can really pick 'em, Ben whispers.

Her pulse bangs and clatters. Her vision starts to blur, and Jacob Vass looms over her, leering, while Ben gurgles blood at her feet.

She sucks in a breath. The icy air slashes the inside of her nose, her throat. Her eyesight sharpens, and it's Caleb standing before her while Elijah drools blood on the snow.

"I thought you knew," Elijah wheezes. "I thought you understood, because you're like me."

Sarah stares down at the guileless boy with his cold, clever hands. Because she does understand. Two peas in a pod. They're both survivors.

And killers.

"You've been protecting him all this time," she says to Caleb.

Protecting him from the law, and from his own urges. From Jacob Vass's legacy of violence.

"I never lied about that."

"Why didn't you turn him in?"

"He's my brother. He's all I have."

Elijah cackles, spitting blood over his father's shearling coat. "All you're left with."

Caleb closes his eyes briefly, and his hands close into fists at his side. "I'm responsible for him. It's all my fault."

"You couldn't have known when you left Sweetside your dad would—"

"No," Caleb says. "It's not that. I'm responsible for who he is. I *made* him."

"Ask him how it felt," Elijah says. His left eye is starting to darken again. "Ask him how it felt to kill Dad. *Who would've thought the old man to have had so much blood in him?*"

Sarah locks eyes with Caleb. His Adam's apple bobs as he struggles to speak, and she reads the truth in his stricken face. He murdered their father, and now Elijah likes to replay the ritual, hungry for a taste of it.

I wanted him to get up so I can hit him again, she'd said.

Oh, she understands Elijah very well.

And then she runs.

That is, she tries to run. Caleb seizes her wrist. Her left wrist, which is still tender from Ben's hand. "Sarah," Caleb rasps. Ben had said her name too, both times, practically growled it. A dark fury flares under her skin.

She pulls out the knife and plunges it into Caleb.

In the middle of nowhere, no one can hear Sarah scream. No one can hear the hum of the blade slipping past wool and into muscle. No one can hear Elijah's laughing or his snort as he gasps wetly.

"Look what you've become," Elijah cackles. "You hurt me. And her. He wins. Dad wins, Caleb."

No one can hear Caleb's strangled grunt or Sarah's cry as he releases her wrist. Triumphant, she sprints toward the road to the Suicide Motel.

Elijah had been right. She *did* enjoy the look of surprise on Caleb's face.

Sarah tries to remember what freedom feels like. But all she can think of is the elation that surged through her when she swung those antlers and gored Ben. The giddy knowledge he would never lie to her again, and his look of disbelief as he gurgled his last breath.

She clings to that joy as she approaches the Suicide Motel. The highway is visible from the parking lot, the ground vibrating beneath her feet from the occasional tanker truck rumbling by. The motel is boarded up, plywood tucked where there should've been glass. Caleb painted over the slur, but she knows it's there. Something that ugly isn't easily covered up by a fresh coat of paint.

Ben's rental car is camouflaged by half a foot of snow, stacked on top like cake icing. The door is unlocked. Of course. Caleb would have made sure it supported the story that Ben abandoned the car for the woods. Sarah slides into the driver's seat, tossing her backpack in the back, praying she can start the cold engine before Caleb reaches her. He's staggering toward the parking lot in the distance. She's relieved the knife blow wasn't fatal—she's left enough bodies behind in Sweetside—but she can't be blamed for anything that happens next. Anger stains her euphoria at getting away. It's Caleb's own fault. He should've come with her when she'd asked. *Look what you did. It doesn't have to be like this.*

She sticks the key in the ignition, as swiftly as she'd slid the knife into Caleb. The dashboard lights up, and she starts the windshield wipers to brush away the worst of the snow. The rubber blades squeal a protest, but there's no time to get out with the ice scraper. She turns the key and the car sputters, begging for a gentle warm-up. It'll have no such luck. She'll have to burn rubber and hope the cold engine can keep up.

Caleb's close enough that she can see him shouting in the rearview mirror. She turns the key again with a determined grunt. Nothing can stop her now, not even Caleb's pretty blue eyes and her name in his pleading mouth.

Nothing except the black-and-white police cruiser that squeals off the highway and comes to a stop in the entrance of the lot.

Sarah's pulse rattles as violently as the car's engine. The cruiser's high beams flick on. She freezes, putting up a hand to shield her eyes from the light.

A door opens, and slams. Officer Isaac is backlit, and Sarah can make out the raised, straight line of his arm and the black service revolver at the end. The rental car engine coughs, and dies, taking the last of her hopes with it.

Isaac approaches the driver's side and opens the door. The gun and his steely gaze never waver. Sarah slowly raises her hands, shaking from the cold and adrenaline and terror.

"Well, well," he drawls. "Miss Sarah. Good thing I decided to check out the mystery car idling in the parking lot. Get out, please."

She obeys, because what else can she do. He's law enforcement, and she's an *Oriental* from the big bad city. She knows how that story ends.

Stumbling footfalls sound behind her, and the gun jumps upward. "Caleb," Isaac says. "You were supposed to keep her contained. I'm disappointed in you, son. Both of you. Up to the house, now."

"Uncle Isaac," Caleb says, voice strained and his face pale and clammy. He puts up his hands. The left arm rises a little slower than the right. There's a slash low in the shoulder of his coat, but no knife hilt. "Don't be hard on Sarah. It's my fault. I told her she could go."

Caleb's eyebrows draw together, and his apologetic smile doesn't betray how much pain he must be in. It strikes Sarah that he also has to act *nice* to survive. Because he's afraid of becoming his father. Afraid of Jacob Vass's ghost, looking out from his eyes, the way Ben has started to look out from hers.

She has as much in common with Caleb as she does with Elijah.

"That doesn't matter. You're both compromised now." Isaac motions to the house with the gun. "Two weeks, at least. You know the rules. Walk, and no funny business. If I have to choose between you and the rest of the town, you know who I'll pick."

Caleb nods. "Yes, sir."

They start the trudge back up to the house, Sarah too numb and scared to speak. Sweetside Manor looms up ahead, and she accepts at last it will not let her go until she's served her time.

Ben's voice in her head laughs and laughs.

Or maybe it's Elijah. He staggers to his feet as they approach, eyes glittering behind his bruises. Isaac *tsks* at him. "Not wearing a mask either, I see. Go on inside, Elijah." He doesn't mention Elijah's swelling face or the blood oozing around his nose and mouth. Elijah picks up his duffel and joins Sarah and Caleb on the death march to the house.

Isaac pulls out his cell phone and picks out a contact, his gun still trained on them. The space between Sarah's shoulder blades tickles. "Jerry? Got a car at the motel that needs towing. Looks like it's been abandoned." He pauses, and heaves a sigh. "No, the motel is *not* cursed. Obviously someone wanted to ditch their car and vanish. Don't go spreading rumors. Also gonna need your help with Sweetside Manor. Round up all the guys you can. Get the table saw from Murry and bring extra plywood and tools if you got 'em. No, be nice. They're cooperating."

Isaac hangs up, and slams the open door of the pickup truck closed as he passes. Sarah flinches at the noise, convinced he'd discharged his gun. She reaches the front porch, mouth sour with dread and the spot between her shoulder blades itching.

"Inside," Isaac says.

Elijah pushes the front door open, and the hinges shriek a welcome. "I'd lock your door," is the last thing Isaac says before the door swings shut behind them.

Caleb gingerly peels off his coat, revealing a dark stain spread over his flannel shirt. Elijah sniffles. His nose bleeds sluggishly, and he cradles his right hand to his belly. Although his downtrodden air may be another act, Sarah can't help responding. She gently wraps him in a hug. He whimpers and rests his head on her shoulder. She doesn't tell him she's sorry. Because she's not. They're two peas in a pod, and he would have betrayed her in an instant, too. He knows this; he sees her like no one else ever has. They see each other now.

She smells blood and cedar and turpentine, and it feels like home.

Caleb circles his arms around them both, and she closes her eyes and leans into his strength. "I'm sorry," he says. Like her, he likes to apologize for things that aren't his fault. He's also a killer who has to hide his true nature.

Entwined with the Vass brothers, she knows she belongs in this gloomy old house and its hunger for dead things, its inhabitants haunted by ghosts. Here, she doesn't have to pretend she's not haunted, too. It hurts to pretend.

"How can we go back to where we were?" Caleb whispers into her hair.

CHAPTER SIXTEEN

You and Caleb sit in the main bathroom with the first aid kit. His face whitens from the pain, but he shows you how to sew up his shoulder. You're pleased that your stitches come out small and neat. Elijah isn't the only one with cold, clever fingers.

Downstairs, the house buzzes from the drone of a table saw. Nails and men's harsh voices hammer into the walls. The light begins to vanish from the ground-floor windows, like stars winking out. At least they're not going to touch the sunroom; they've only blocked the side door with an empty dumpster. You just won't look out that way. You can still admire the woods through the plastic. And you can sit on the loveseat and watch Elijah paint. His sprained fingers will eventually heal, but in the meantime, he'll teach himself to hold a paintbrush in his left hand.

You kiss Caleb and help him button up his shirt. Something downstairs smells delicious, so you both head to the kitchen. Elijah has already set the table. Isaac's wife Judy has dropped off a pot roast, handed through the gap they left in the boards over the front door. It sits on the kitchen table, steaming, with your cleaned paring knife stuck in it. The knife is small, but it's sharp, and anyway, it's the only knife in the house.

Elijah's eye is swollen shut, and the open neck of his shirt displays Ben's bruises like a necklace. The gift of a dead man. No, a *disappeared* man. At night, you'll lie awake in Caleb's arms and hear Ben screaming with the others in the woods. He doesn't whisper in your head anymore, because it was your voice all along.

When the two weeks are up and they take down the plywood, you know you will stay at Sweetside Manor. You're finally free here. Caleb will keep you safe, and the two of you keep Elijah safe. Beautiful Elijah, with the face of an angel and the soul of a killer. You know, because you share the same soul.

Uncle Isaac will come by asking about Ben, and the three of you will tell him he paid his dues to the Suicide Motel. Ben's family will be unsurprised, and the investigation will end there. They'll retrieve his grey coat, and Ben's mother will ask if you want to keep it. Sometimes you'll put it on like you're wearing his skin, like Elijah wears Jacob Vass's shearling. It won't smell like him anymore. It'll smell of the woods.

When the snow thaws, you and Caleb will plant what's left of Ben out back. Or maybe in the foundation of a new extension on the house, extending from the parlor. You'll pick out paint swatches and put up drywall. It'll be nice to work with your hands again. You'll keep the plastic slipcovers on Grandma Sweet's sofa, however. It makes it easier to clean.

When the vaccine rolls out and restrictions lift, you'll help Caleb write the guest wing's description on Airbnb, and Elijah will show tourists where to hike and fish. Graham will even visit, but you'll let him leave unharmed. He did try to rescue you, after all, before you knew you belonged here.

And sometimes you will tell dangerous men with storms inside them that the woods scream at night, but it's all right, they can scream back and no one will hear. No one except you and Elijah and the knives you're not supposed to have.

But at this moment, the three of you take your places at the table, around the pot roast and green beans and mashed potatoes. You know you will never leave the Vass brothers, and they will never leave you. Caleb takes your hand, and you know he loves you. And fears you. As much as you love and fear him. Elijah takes your other hand. Squeezes it tightly. You smile at him. He trembles a little. He's as scared of your bland smile as you fear his soulful eyes. Such a beautiful boy. So beautiful, so sweet. But rotten on the inside. Just like you. You belong together.

You wonder if anyone can see you through the windows, even though they're almost finished boarding them up. You wonder if any of the townspeople are peeping through the cracks right now at the city girl and the strange brothers who run the Suicide Motel. It's too bad if they aren't.

They'll never know what a beautiful family you are. If they knew, they would love and fear you, too.

"Let us give thanks," you say.

THE END

ACKNOWLEDGMENTS

Although this novella was written at the height of the COVID-19 lockdown, it was not a solitary endeavor. I owe a debt to two courses from the late LitReactor website: Gemma Files's Write What You Fear, and Gwenda Bond's Getting it Done. They helped me, well, write what I feared, and get it done. Many thanks to Carolyn Charron for beta reading, my agent Dorian Maffei for her guidance, and Lee Murray and Holly Lyn Walrath for plucking this novella from the slush pile. Most of all, much love and gratitude to the friends I kept online company with during the pandemic: Kari, Rati, KT, Phoebe, Ariella, Charlotte, Rob, Christina, Janine, Jess, Amy, Allison, Alyx, and Kelly. I'd help every one of you bury the bodies.

ABOUT THE AUTHOR

E. L. Chen is the author of *The Good Brother* and *Summerwood/Winterwood*, the latter of which was longlisted for the Sunburst and recommended as a Best Book for Kids and Teens by the Canadian Children's Book Centre. Her short fiction has been published in venues such as *Strange Horizons, On Spec, Lackington's,* and *The Dark*. She lives in Toronto, Canada with her son.

INTERSTELLAR FLIGHT PRESS

Interstellar Flight Press is an indie speculative publishing house. We feature innovative works from the best new writers in science fiction and fantasy. In the words of Ursula K. Le Guin, we need "writers who can see alternatives to how we live now, can see through our fear-stricken society and its obsessive technologies to other ways of being, and even imagine real grounds for hope."

Find us online at www.interstellarflightpress.com.

 facebook.com/InterstellarFlightPress
 instagram.com/interstellarflightpress
bsky.app/profile/interstellarflight.bsky.social

www.ingramcontent.com/pod-product-compliance
Lightning Source LLC
LaVergne TN
LVHW040103080526
838202LV00045B/3757